Change In Course

Mark Raffles

DEDICATION

This book is dedicated to all the true friends I've ever had, especially my best friend, Cathy.

1

April, 2008

Frank Jordan had never been fired before.

"The firm is moving in a different direction," Cliff Magro said, in the modern way of saying you would no longer be receiving a paycheck. "This in no way is a reflection on your abilities or the job you have done."

Of course it's a reflection on my abilities and the job I've done, Frank thought. Otherwise you wouldn't be firing me. He wanted to say that, but remained silent.

Magro continued. "We have a generous severance package for you, and you can count on me to help you in any way I can."

After a moment of awkward silence Frank realized it was his turn to talk.

"This is a shock," he lied.

Frank could tell Magro was carefully judging which way this meeting would go. Would Frank scream at him and stomp out, vowing to unleash lawyers on the firm? That would embarrass them both, but since only Magro would be in the office the next day, he had more to lose in that scene. Or would Frank become argumentative, clinging to a sliver of hope that his fate wasn't already sealed, that there was a chance he could somehow reverse the forces that were pushing him out the door? Or, God forbid, would Frank break down and cry right there in the office, the same one in which they'd celebrated previous successes, saluting their brilliance together?

Frank thought it ironic that he was the author of how this scene played out, even though he was the one getting the axe. He suddenly became aware that there was no Human Resources person present, and, to his amusement, no security guard. He chalked both of those facts up to Magro's ego, that he wanted the rest of the office to know that he could handle this unpleasant task without help. Frank wondered if Magro thought he could get away with that because of their relationship, or because he fancied himself a great manager. No one in the office thought that was true.

They had worked together for 8 years, after Magro had been hired as portfolio manager from GreatBank, and Frank's ability as a stock analyst to find overlooked value in smaller companies had helped them post excellent returns together. For his part, Magro had a knack for leveraging his bets at just the right point in the stock market cycle, and the resulting superior performance in his clients' accounts had led to him being named office manager 3 years ago. It was an easy call for senior management in New York to promote Magro, since portfolio managers are more highly valued than analysts and Frank was only one of several analysts that had contributed to the fund's success. While he didn't exactly consider Magro a friend, they had worked very closely together, attended plenty of Wall Street-sponsored golf outings and ball games, and were a little more than just co-workers.

"I'm really sorry about this. It's just a head count issue and New York makes that call," Magro said.

Frank knew deep down that Magro was just a little afraid of what Frank might do, and he saw his opening. It wouldn't amount to much, but at least he could remember the moment as one in which he took his best shot.

"So Ed makes some numbers on a piece of paper look better to Jack, and Ed makes another hundred thousand dollars, and Jack makes another two fifty. Oh, and when management announces the layoffs, and the associated savings from them, the stock will go up. I know how it works, Marc. I'm an analyst, remember? I used to be the person praising companies that cut expenses," Frank said.

Now I'm on the receiving end, he thought.

"I don't know if that's what's going on here," Magro said, averting his eyes to the window. "It's a horrible economy and things are bad here. They have to make some changes. You understand that."

Frank noticed that Magro had said "they," "they have to make some changes," not "we." He shook his head. It was the classic modern method of firing someone, trying to get them to see the company's point of view, as if that would make a difference in the life of the person getting axed. It also showed a certain condescension, the questioning of whether the axed employee could "understand" the reasoning behind their firing. Frank was having none of it.

"Nothing's changing for you. Or Ed, or Jack. The only thing really changing is that tomorrow, I don't have a way to make a paycheck."

"The severance package will help you until you get back on your feet. I was impressed by it, by the way. Much more generous that I thought it would be."

Like it matters that the little numbers on a page were

impressive to you, Frank thought. It was just more condescension, the idea that the company is generously giving the fired person more than is deserved. There's one thing about business firings that hasn't changed in 50 years, or maybe even longer: one human being is sitting across a desk from another human being, telling them they could no longer show up at that place to trade their labor for money. Oh, the details have been adjusted, maybe. Now it probably takes place in a glass office tower, with severance pay, and the promise of outplacement services. But the result is no different than when it happened in the factory floor manager's office, with steel file cases and linoleum flooring. The next day, life would only be different for one of them. That person would wake up the next day with no money coming in, and then have to go out and convince another person at another company to let them come in every day and earn a paycheck.

At this point Frank figured that if wanted to, he could play on Magro's conscience to make him work harder for the harmonious resolution that Magro so badly wanted, but he saw no reason to prolong the sorry episode just for his own amusement. He'd said his piece.

"What happens now?"

Magro seemed surprised by the change in direction, and scrambled to look through the folder in front of him. "Well, uh, let's see. You need to go down to HR, uh, I guess they have a procedure they go through, and, uh, they have an envelope with all the details."

He looked up at Frank and with fake sincerity said, "Frank, I will help you in any way I can. You know that."

Frank stood up. Magro hesitated a second and then quickly followed suit. It was clear that Frank had seized the moment, and Magro scrambled to make sure he didn't look submissive. Magro ran through a checklist in his head. Had he shown weakness by allowing the meeting to be cut short? Had he presented the company's stance, while showing empathy toward the employee?

Frank knew he had won the battle, but had lost the war.

"Thanks," Frank said curtly, and turned to walk out.

Magro hurried around the desk and tried to meet Frank at the door. They'd worked together for 8 years, but like all business, in the end it's every man for himself.

There was a brief moment when Magro realized he was now close enough for Frank to punch, and he pulled back just enough for so that both of them realized that possibility. Capitalizing on the opportunity, Frank made just a subtle move towards his now former boss, just enough to elicit a little fear in his eyes, and instead reached for the doorknob. Seeing no reason for a handshake, he opened the door and walked out.

August, 1970

Paul Smith thought most things in life were stupid, and in this case he was right.

His platoon had already been down this crappy Mekong Delta road twice this week and found nothing, and making him walk it again with all the gear and ammo in the morning heat held no apparent purpose other than making him hot and tired.

He had a hard time these days remembering when he wasn't miserable. After being in country for 7 months and 5 days he thought it best to stay sharp. He didn't consider himself a short-timer yet, but he'd seen too many guys get killed when they started to think about home too often and too early.

For Paul, home was Eastridge, Illinois, a big suburb just north of Chicago. Like most teenagers, he had found life kind of boring. He'd played sports with his friends, watched black and white television, tried to obtain beer - all the typical things suburban boys did. It wasn't so much that he joined the Army for excitement; he just hadn't liked his other options at the time. He didn't consider himself the college type, and he wasn't quite ready to trudge to a factory every morning.

Kasten was walking eight paces ahead of him, and Lauer was behind him. Traipsing down the dirt road in the heat with a group of guys caused his mind to wander back to August high school football practices. He recalled the feeling of shared misery, going through endless drills with bulky equipment, and wishing that he was somewhere else.

Then the shooting started.

Paul could tell that right away that a few guys had been hit because he was familiar with the unique sound that a bullet makes when it hits flesh and bone. He jumped off the road to his right and returned fire into a tree line about 75 yards away. The grass was about three feet tall so he had a little cover but looked around for something else to get behind. The road was elevated about three feet, and it took him about 30 seconds to realize he had jumped to the wrong side of it.

He looked around to see who was up. Kasten had jumped off the road to the other side, and he was now also firing at the tree line, using the dirt road as cover. Paul looked back down the road and couldn't make anyone out, including Lauer. The firing seemed heavier there, so the ambush had hit when the platoon was far enough down the road to be out in the open. He heard a couple screams back there, too, and was gripped by the fear that he was the last guy in the line still firing. He had to get across the road.

There were two choices: wait for the VC shooting to let up and crouch-sprint across the road, or crawl across under fire and hope the gooks weren't advancing through the grasses right now. That decision was made for him when

7

the LT yelled, "DD now!" and he saw GIs humping through the taller grasses on the other side of the road away from him as fast as possible.

Paul continued firing backwards, staying as low to the ground as possible, and stumbled to the other side of the road and kept on going. The ground was a little soft and uneven, and it was tricky to keep from falling while running as fast as he could. It reminded him of the wind sprints he'd run during high school football after the rains hit the practice field. Of course, back then it was a lark, he and his friends in their orange and navy blue Eastridge uniforms. Now men wanted to kill him. He had never been this afraid.

He could just see glimpses of other GIs running through the tall grasses, including Kasten to his right, but saw no one to his left. That wasn't good. He came over a slight rise, bending over to stay low. On the downslope his foot caught on something soft and he fell forward on his face. What the hell did I step on? he thought. As he scrambled to his feet he turned to see.

It was Edwards, a tall, thin black kid from Detroit. He and Paul had talked about cars a few times. "Help me, man," he pleaded.

Paul had a quick mind. He could continue running and have a much better chance of making it out. If he did get shot in the back and killed what would it matter that he was on his own as opposed to getting killed trying to help another soldier? If Paul made it out, and Edwards surely wouldn't without his help, would the decision to leave him there haunt him? Or would he not care because he was alive? Edwards was wounded; would he die anyway and needlessly cost Paul his own life?

Paul dumped his pack and looked Edwards over. He had taken hits in his right thigh and upper arm. If Paul could get him out of there he stood a chance to make it. He had to take him. He pulled Edwards over to him and bent down like a weightlifter to hoist him over his shoulders. He was a little lighter than Paul had expected.

The firing behind him had not let up, and in his mind, the VC were sprinting through the grasses behind him and would take him down any second. The adrenaline was still pumping, but after running with Edwards about 50 yards he could feel his body start to tire. Despair crept into his head. Is this it? He thought. Am I going to die in this Godforsaken field thousands of miles from home, carrying this guy on my back? For just a split second that thought sent a new type of fear through him, but there was nothing else to do but to keep on running.

He ran another 50 yards and could feel the fire in his lungs. He could dump Edwards right here and no one would ever know. But he kept on putting one foot in front of the other, and heard Edwards grunt something that Paul couldn't make it out. He didn't have the breath to spare to ask him to repeat it. Edwards grunted again.

"Choppers, man!"

Edwards was pointing to Paul's right where one Huey had landed about 60 yards away and other was about to set down 30 yards closer.

Paul figured the second chopper would set down right about when he arrived and he was right. He was 6 steps from the door when the Huey's M60 machine gun opened up over his left shoulder. It was so close he ducked down and thought he could hear the lead whizzing by. He was just a step away from the open door when he saw the Huey's runner start to lift up off the ground. He tossed Edwards into the chopper, put a foot on the runner and dove in just as the helicopter lifted up. He grabbed the strap on the floor and held on as the chopper swung around and headed off.

Paul looked down to where he'd just left the clearing and saw five or six VC lying in the grass where the M60 had just ripped them up. They had indeed been very close, and now that he saw them freshly dead he felt cold and faint. He dropped his head on the chopper's floor and looked up at the machine gunner.

The gunner looked at him and gave him a smile that said, "You're welcome."

3

July, 1977

The hostess smiled and picked up two menus. "Your table is ready."

Walking behind Rachel Conrad on their first date, Barry Stone noticed her great figure but small stature. He had always had a fondness for a gymnast's build, and she certainly had that. If things worked out with her, and they had children, they'd be great looking, although the height gene would still be missing in the Stone hereditary line.

Stop thinking like that, you idiot, he thought. It's only your first date. But he was very much hoping things would work out - he'd had a major crush on Rachel since their days at the University of Illinois.

The hostess showed them to a table by the window, overlooking the Chicago River. "Enjoy," she said, before returning to the podium. Rachel leaned over the table. "I've really wanted to try this place," she said.

"It's gotten great reviews."

As she settled back to look over the menu Barry couldn't help sneaking glances at her over his menu. God, he thought, Rachel was so beautiful. She had jet black hair that she continually pulled behind her ear, dark brown eyes, and a smile where her lower lip paused just a split second before falling below her teeth. That little hesitation stopped Barry's heart every time.

"So, you work at a clothing wholesaler at the Merchandise Mart? That sounds really interesting," he offered.

"I really like it. Everyone there is so nice and you meet a lot of interesting people. Ralph Lauren came in last week. He talked to me about his line, and asked me what I thought of it," she said.

"Ralph Lauren? Really? That's so cool."

"Like I'm going to tell Ralph Lauren, 'Oh, this color doesn't really work.' Yeah, sure." She smiled, and her lower lip did the hesitation step. Magic. "So tell me about your life. How's the job?"

"Well, I'm at Ernst and Young, mostly doing auditing work. They send us into companies, and we set up shop for a few weeks, or sometimes months, and go over their books, you know, looking for discrepancies." He paused. "I guess that sounds pretty boring."

"No, not if you like it. You know, my dad has an accounting firm."

"So you're used to boring."

"Oh, no. I love my dad. He's not boring."

"No, no, I didn't mean anything by that," Barry stumbled. "I just mean some people think accounting is THE most boring job on the planet." She's touchy about her dad, remember that, Barry thought.

"How long have you lived at Irving and Lake Shore?" Rachel asked, clearly changing the subject.

"About a year. My friend and I, he's another accountant – I know, I really sound dull now – we love the location. We can run along the Drive, walk to Wrigley Field, and Waveland Golf Course is right across the street. It only costs 4 bucks for nine holes."

"Isn't that the course that runs right along the Drive? Don't balls go flying into cars?"

Barry laughed. "Actually it is, and they do. I was playing with a guy one time and he sliced 3 balls onto Lake Shore Drive before he gave it up. It was hilarious."

The waiter came by, introduced himself as Ian, and took their drink order.

"So you live with another accountant, and play golf? You're quite the exciting guy, Barry," Rachel said. Again she flashed that disarming smile.

"All right, all right. So what do you like to do?"

"I like going to these little theatres in town. Not the big productions downtown, but there's some amazing acting in these little out-of-the-way venues. It's so fun."

"That does sound fun. I'd love to go to a play sometime." He dropped the hint for a second date.

Before she could respond Ian returned with their drinks and his recital of the specials. Rachel ordered the shrimp scampi and Barry the ravioli.

"What kind of music do you like?" he asked.

"Well, let's see. I like Stevie Wonder, I absolutely LOVE Fleetwood Mac, I like Rod Stewart…"

"I like Rod Stewart's older stuff, you know, *Maggie May*, and *I'm Losing You*. That stuff," Barry said.

"Really? I'm more into his newer songs. What about Elton John?"

"He's good. I like *Your Song*, and *Rocket Man*."

"So his older stuff." Rachel smiled. "I think I see a pattern here."

Barry smiled back, but wished he could rewind the conversation like a cassette tape. "Maybe we better talk about movies."

"The best movie I saw this year was *Annie Hall*. I couldn't stop laughing. Did you see it?" she asked.

"I did. I really…"

"Wait, don't tell me. You like Woody Allen's older films better, right?"

They continued getting to know each other, talking about the transition from college to first real jobs, from suburban houses to city apartments. The distance hadn't been too far for either of them. Rachel had grown up in Glenbrook, a suburb just a little northwest of Eastridge, and had studied marketing at Illinois. They were the first wave of baby boomers, moving into the city to taste the urban life that their parents had fled. While Chicago in the late '70s was still gritty, the areas where young college graduates were settling was still a far cry from the neighborhoods that their parents had come from.

After dinner, Barry excused himself and made towards the men's room, hoping to find Ian the waiter near the bar, far from their table. Unfortunately the restaurant was too busy, so Barry was forced to have the conversation only three tables over from where Rachel sat. He positioned himself between their table and Ian.

"I have 2 certificates for half off the entrees." Barry kept his voice low. The bill had been almost three times what he had expected, as he'd tried to impress Rachel with an expensive bottle of wine.

Ian reacted as Barry had feared. "I'm sorry, sir. You can only use one certificate per meal. I think that's written on the back." He placed a beer down on the table in front of a patron.

"Yes, that's true. But if we had ordered separate checks then we meet the requirements."

Ian moved to his left and placed the bill on another table. "I'll take this when you're ready," he said. He turned back to Barry. "But you didn't order separate checks, and I've already entered your orders."

The conversation was taking longer than he dared and he desperately wanted to avoid raising Rachel's suspicions. Should he just bite the bullet or push harder? He decided to try a different tact – empathy.

"Look, I'm on a first date with this girl I've liked since college. You understand. I brought her here to impress her because this is such a fabulous restaurant. Come on, can't you help me out and take the certificate?" he pleaded.

For the first time Ian gave him his attention. "I don't make the rules. I'm just doing my job. I'd like to help but I can't. Do you want me to get the manager?"

This was not working. The last thing he needed was a scene with the manager at the table. He thought that the evening had gone pretty well and now he was going to blow it. It was a big bill to pay but he was just going to have to swallow it. Plus now he was going to have to explain the long conversation with the waiter.

He felt a tap on his shoulder. Great. Now what?

He turned to find Rachel looking through her purse.

"That bill must be huge. Let's ask for separate checks. I have a certificate for half off the entrée."

She fished out the coupon, handed it to Barry, and smiled, her lower lip pausing just a split second before falling below her teeth.

4

April, 2008

Since Frank had been fired at 10am on a Monday, the usual drive home would only take fifteen minutes rather than the usual 45 it required at rush hour. That didn't give him much time to figure out how to break the news to Kate Jordan.

The meeting with Barbara, the human relations woman, had gone a little better than he had expected. He would receive six month's pay, with benefits, outplacement services, and a severance payment of $45,000. Barbara had seemed very cautious in parsing each word, which Frank assumed was intended to prevent an age discrimination suit from a 57 year old employee being shown the door. The bank had lain off 16 people that day from the investment group, of varying ages, although Frank knew he was the oldest by about 9 years. Frank was not about to enter the legal morass a lawsuit would entail. Only the lawyers profit from that folly, and as Frank looked for a new job, did he really want to be suing his last employer?

He was sure that this decision had been scrutinized for weeks because the bank avoided bad publicity like the plague, which meant that someone, or more likely a few people, had known Frank was on the chopping block for a while. That thought gave him an uneasy feeling.

After the HR meeting had come the hard part – going back to his desk to retrieve his personal items. He figured that everyone on the floor knew what was happening, and who it was happening to. He had never been one to care much about what other people thought, but making his way around the office for the last time today had been uncomfortable. Someone, somewhere, had decided that his labor was not as good as the other people he would have to pass on the way to his desk. Deep down he knew it was much more complicated than that – there was an age and compensation matrix to solve – but as a competitive person it hurt that he had been judged as expendable.

The people he had worked with – who just this morning were co-workers – reacted as he had expected. The younger ones held phones up to their ears, engaging or pretending to engage in conversations that would prevent an awkward interaction with Frank as he passed through. He could see them sneak peeks at him. The ones with more courage made their way over to offer the usual bromides.

"This is unfair. You do great work."

"You should be glad you're out of here. This place sucks."

"You'll have no problem finding another job."

Frank thanked each one for the sentiment, if not the content, of their comments and quickly packed his photos, a few momentos like his Ernie Banks-signed baseball, and his framed Chartered Financial Analyst certificate. He had never been so grateful for elevator doors to open, and he exhaled after he climbed onboard and the doors mercifully closed.

You're supposed to fire someone on Friday afternoon, not Monday morning, Frank had thought as he walked to his car. The stupid bank can't even do that right. But at least it made his last drive home easier.

He had been a financial analyst for 31 years, the last twelve at First Fidelity. He'd been good - but not great - at recommending stocks for the bank's mutual fund managers to invest in, and was well-liked by the other analysts, portfolio managers, and traders. He was well-liked by Magro, too, but the decision to terminate him had been made far above that level in the company. Although the layoffs were couched in terms of the need for headcount reduction in light of the financial crisis and the bank's horrible operating results, he could see the pattern in who had been let go and who hadn't. It was no coincidence that the ones who had kept their jobs tended to be lower paid. You can only spin things so far – the bank was clearly cutting higher paid employees.

Kate's car was not in the garage when he pulled in. She wouldn't be home for a while from Jefferson Elementary school, where she spent hours of time as a low-paid teacher's aide. Counting all the extra hours she put in there Frank figured she averaged less than minimum wage, but it gave her a great sense of joy to be involved and she truly loved the children. She'd started at Jefferson when their oldest, Nate, was a high school sophomore, and he was now 26 and on his own. Besides, they had not needed the money. Maybe that would change.

Frank sat down on the couch and reflexively flicked on the TV. His Blackberry had been buzzing for an hour now but he hadn't been in the mood to interact with anyone. He looked at the screen now and saw he had 20 messages broken down this way: 5 missed calls, 11 emails, and 4 texts. Perhaps he would be able to rank how much each of his friends cared by their method of contact, he mused.

After a few minutes of quickly clicking through his midday viewing options (The Munsters, Oprah, Sportscenter, an old Western) he landed on MSNBC, but then immediately turned it off. He felt a little twinge of fear, realizing he was no longer part of the financial world, and it might be some time – or never – before he would rejoin it.

At about 3pm he heard Kate come in from the garage. She was in her usual good spirits but naturally wondering why he was home. She set her purse on the counter and sat down on the other couch facing Frank. "Not feeling well, honey?"

"You know how I told you this downturn was going to cause a lot of people to lose their jobs?"

"Oh, no," Kate said, not in an alarmed way, more in a sympathetic tone.

"Yes, you are looking at the latest victim."

Kate got up and moved over beside him, draping his arm over her shoulder. "I'm so sorry. What did they say?"

"Does it matter? It's all the usual nonsense about the firm, and the economy, and blah blah blah. In the end it means nothing except that I'm out of work."

"Can you talk to Ed in New York? He always liked you."

"Ed cares about Ed. They're all nice to you until it starts to affect their own paycheck. Then it's every man for himself."

Kate wrapped her arms around him. "So what are you going to do?"

"Well, they gave me $45,000 severance pay, and six month's salary, so we'll be okay for a while. I'll start making some calls tomorrow. Right now I'm just going to sit here, watch television, and feel sorry for myself."

Kate smiled. "Okay, I'll do that with you."

He sat down next to him on the couch and for the moment, everything in Frank's world was all right. He'd leave it until tomorrow to start worrying.

5

Paul walked back up to the house from his red Candor Electric van carrying two styles of light dimming switches. The customer, Julie Adamcyzk, was a tall divorcee with a big smile and a small budget, updating her kitchen lighting, which Paul figured dated from the 1950s.

As he outlined her dimmer choices for the light over the kitchen table, he noticed her showing a great deal more interest than dimmers merited.

"The bar makes it easy to manipulate the lighting level, but you might prefer just an on/off switch with a wheel to regulate the lighting level," he said.

"What is your recommendation?" she asked.

"It's all personal choice. I install a lot of these wheels. People seem to like them."

"Yes, I see. It's a matter of personal choice." She said, smiling.

Working the Chicago suburbs as an electrician, Paul had been in this spot many times before. The married women usually were just looking for attention; a little flirting with the handsome blue collar electrician before their high-earning husband, who deep down the women really believed they deserved to be with, returned home.

Some of the married ones were willing to take it a little bit further, maybe dance a little closer to the flame, and Paul usually avoided those. On the rare occasion when he hadn't pulled away, when he'd let it go a little farther than he should have, it had felt wrong, like he had allowed himself to turn to the dark side just a little bit.

The divorced women were a different story. Paul had always had an easy manner with women, and he prided himself on maintaining his looks. He still had his hair, now graying and cut tight to his head, and he was about 6 foot two inches tall, with a lean physique credited to good genes, but he also had a solid workout ethic picked up during those summer high school football practices years ago. It was not a surprise that he caught the eye of many a divorcee as he knelt down to repair their wiring or stood on a ladder to add floodlights on their driveways. He figured that being divorced himself gave him special insight into their thinking, and that the combination of once having had the experience of real intimacy with a marriage partner, but now being a free agent, seemed to create an easy connection. Maybe it was also the common bond that they had both failed at the same thing.

He considered himself a moral person, and a professional workman, and on those occasions that he had found himself attracted to someone he had always asked them out on a proper date. Sure, there had been a few instances when he gave in to a little animal passion during the day, but nothing more permanent ever came of those episodes. He had turned down some kinky requests, and was sure some of them would've gone even beyond what he imagined.

"You seem particularly interested in dimmers, Ms. Adamcyzk," Paul said, returning her smile.

"Call me Julie."

6

Barry found himself engaged in another inane conversation, this one with the brake shop manager. Why did this keep happening to him?

"I'm sorry, Mr. Stone. The promotion is only good for one axle per visit."

Barry could hardly hear him over the phone with the air hammers in the background. "Yes I understand. But you told me I need new brakes for both axles?"

"Yes, that's right."

"So if I did the front axle today, and the rear axle tomorrow I could get the sale price on both?"

"Correct."

"Or, I could get the front axle done in the morning, and the rear axle done in the afternoon. Then I would qualify for the sale price, right?"

The manager still didn't see where this was headed. "Um, I guess."

"So if I got the front axle done right now, and then drove the car out of your shop, and then pulled back in, that would be a separate visit, no?"

That one caused a pause at the other end of the phone. Finally, the man replied, "That's not really the idea."

Barry sensed his opening. "Okay. Well, I think the idea is to get people into your shop to get their brakes done, and see what good work you guys do. That's exactly what I'm doing. It's just that I happen to need both axles done. So, rather than take my car down off the jacks, drive around the block, and then pull back into your shop, why don't you just pretend I did that and do both axles for the sale price?"

"That's not the idea."

"But the idea is to get more business, right? This is more business."

"It's one axle per visit."

"Do you really want me to tell my wife to pay for one axle, drive around the block, and then pull in again?"

There was silence, then a resigned sigh at the other end of the phone. "Okay, Mr. Stone. I'll give you the discount."

"Thanks. I appreciate it."

As he hung up the phone Barry knew his wife Rachel would not have been happy if she had had to drive the car around the block to get the discount. Rachel Stone was already unhappy about having to take in Barry's car today. But then again, Rachel seemed unhappy about almost everything these days.

Despite all the outward trappings of success - the big house in Highmoor, the membership at Bellwood Country Club, - underlying everything these days was a growing irritation Rachel seemed to have regarding almost everything Barry did. Most times it was subtle, but more recently it appeared as almost disdain. Their sons, Derek and Wes, were on their own now, achieving their own success, and the vacuum they had left in the Stone house had yet to be filled. Barry assumed it was typical for there to be a period of adjustment as Rachel found new activities to focus on, but the unhappiness seemed to linger. Now he wondered if something else was involved. Or someone else.

Barry's admin called. "Mr. Stone, Mr. Conrad needs you."

He grabbed a pen and notebook and walked down the corridor to Dean Conrad's office. Barry had joined his father-in-law's accounting firm 21 years ago, assuming that eventually Dean would yield the reins to him, but at age 78 Dean showed no signs of giving up anything.

The relationship had always been just a little off – Dean had always been a doting grandparent to the boys, but with Barry he had kept a more aloof approach, even after all these years. And at work he was even standoffish, maintaining a well-defined boss/employee dynamic. In fact, Barry was never quite sure where he stood with Dean, despite being generally regarded as the number 2 man at the fifteen accountant firm, and he was certain Dean relished that sense of uncertainty.

Barry walked into Dean's office and sat across the desk. As usual, Dean continued to read the piece of paper he was holding just a little longer than necessary, making Barry wait. Then he tossed the paper across the desk to Barry.

"Capitol Paint is late again, both with their U107 forms and their check. You can't keep letting that happen."

Barry picked up the paper and pretended to read it. He knows that Capitol has only been late twice, and he knows I know it, too, he thought. Lots of accounts were much later with reports and checks. There was more to it than this. Something else was brewing. He had a chilling thought. Did this nonsense have something to do with the problems he was having with Rachel. Could it go that deep?

"Yes, this is bad. I'll take care of it," Barry said. He stood up, trying to get out of there as quickly as possible.

"Hang on a second, Barry. I have something else." Dean removed his glasses. After a few awkward seconds he said, "I'm going to shift the Jackson-Hoyt account over to Fred. He's a little underused now since Alliance Pharma screwed us and left and I think it fits better with his account portfolio."

Jackson-Hoyt was Barry's second biggest account, and his favorite. Their sponsorship of PGA golf tournaments allowed Barry to play in Pro-Am events with some of golf's top names, plus he often received state-of-the-art golf equipment.

"Dean, I've known those guys for years. I helped them when they had the Enron problem. I don't think they're going to like the switch. And that's a big account for me."

"You've got plenty of work, and very soon you'll have more administrative duties around here." That was the carrot Dean had dangled before Barry for years, that he would be more involved the small firm's management. But, of course, it had never materialized.

They went back and forth a little more on the account switch, but Barry knew Dean rarely changed his mind. He got up to leave.

"You need to smooth the transition so there's no issues with the Jackson people," Dean said as Barry reached the office door.

Barry nodded. Maybe I will, he thought. Or maybe it's time for a new plan.

7

Northcroft Golf Club had been built in 1947 by Herman "Hy" Macdonald, and it had been owned and operated by the family until 2005. Hy's great grandsons, Billy and Bobby Macdonald, traded their commodities accounts in the morning, and then spent their afternoons at the club, sitting on the patio and drinking, hanging around the clubhouse, and occasionally even playing a round of golf. They were poor golfers, but pretty good commodity traders, and everything was fine until 2005 when the broker they traded through – Refco – suddenly declared bankruptcy due to financial fraud. Faced with an immediate lack of liquid funds, the Macdonalds had to unload assets, including a Vail condo, a piece of a racehorse, and ultimately, Northcroft.

They found a buyer in the Highview Group, some local doctors who envisioned owning a golf course as a fabulous lark. It wasn't, and as the losses piled up they kept cutting corners until the fairways became more brown than green, the greens became more bumpy than smooth, and only about half of the golf carts ran.

The course's biggest loss – figuratively speaking – was

occurring just as Frank Jordan, Paul Smith, and Barry Stone pulled into the parking lot to play a round.

"I've had enough of this!" yelled Tommy G. "I quit!"

Thomas Gianelli's first day at Northcroft had been when he was fresh out of high school in 1968, and since that time he had cut grass, laid sod, moved holes, raked traps, fixed golf carts, and generally kept the course running. When the Macdonalds had owned the place he'd been almost a member of their family, respecting the fact that Tommy knew every inch of Northcroft – where to overseed, which carts were balky, which golfers liked early tee times. He'd essentially run the club since 1985.

But when the doctors took over, well, Tommy was just an older employee, one who always seemed to be in a foul mood over something. It was a battle of wills over whether the lack of maintenance funds would force Tommy to quit before the doctors were forced to sell the course to cut their already large and growing losses. It looked like the issue would be settled today.

"Please, Tommy," pleaded Chris Keller the club's golf professional. He held his hand over the phone and had two calls waiting, as the computer reservations were messed up (again) and the teenage desk clerk hadn't shown up (again). "Don't quit today. The doctors will come through with the sand shipment."

"You say that every week. They don't give a damn that the traps look like razor stubble. It's just a hobby with them," Tommy ranted.

"Hold on just one more second, please," Chris said to the caller. One of the lights on hold went out, signaling another green fee forfeited that they could ill afford to lose.

"Tommy, we'll get the sand. Just don't quit today. Please. We need you."

"Forget it! I've had enough of those clowns! I don't

need this!" Tommy threw up his arms and stormed out of the clubhouse, barely avoiding the three golfers as they entered.

"Be with you in one minute, gentlemen," Chris said as he wrote down the tee time reservation he'd taken over the phone. "Now, what can I do for you?"

"We'd like to play 18, walking," Barry said.

"Okay, I can get you right off. Do you need any balls or tees?"

"No, we're good."

"Paying together or separate?"

"Separate."

"Okay, let me just get that set up here," Chris said. After a few frustrating minutes of tapping the keyboard and grimacing, he finally said, "You know, I'm having some computer issues here. Why don't you just tee off and pay when you come in?"

Paul looked raised his eyebrows at Frank, who just shook his head.

"Can you believe what a pit this place has become?" Paul remarked as they walked out to the first tee.

"No kidding," Frank replied. "Was that Tommy G we saw leaving in a hurry?"

"The one and only."

Barry walked slowly behind his friends, his attention drawn to a woman on the driving range launching one beautiful shot after another. She wore a short white skirt, magenta golf top, and a black Titleist cap. She was deliberate in her motion, using the alignment rods to keep on target, and went through the same pre-shot routine so ubiquitous in televised golf tournaments.

"You coming?" Paul asked.

"Watch this swing," Barry replied without taking his eyes off her.

Another graceful seven iron landed softly down the range.

"Impressive. Now let's go."

When they arrived at the first tee a small crowd of middle aged men had gathered to listen to the starter spin tales of past glory.

"So this kid says to me, 'How do I know what a good tackle feels like, Coach D?' So I say, 'Get down in your tackling stance and look straight ahead.' Then I grab me one of them wood boards, you know, the ones we laid on the ground to make sure the kids kept their feet wide apart? Anyway, I pick up the board and smack the kid right in the facemask with it. I say, 'that's what a good tackle feels like!' "

The crowd roared with laughter at football coaching legend Charles "Chick" Demaso. Coach D had spent 32 years at Deer Valley High, with some surprising early success, but eventually, his old school coaching techniques led to a decade or so of ineptitude and parental complaints. The school board finally eased him into retirement, whereupon he found a cushy job at as the Northcroft starter. The Macdonald boys in particular loved to hear the old coach's stories, and believed their manhood was enhanced by their association with him, although they hadn't played football themselves.

As Frank, Paul, and Barry approached the tee box they noticed no one was on the first hole, and no one seemed to be preparing to play, either. Frank walked right up, placed his ball on a tee, and prepared to tee off.

"What do you think you're doing?" Coach D yelled over to him, but remained in his golf cart.

Frank ignored him, but Paul squared up to face him, as well as the group around him. "We're teeing off," he said.

The brief moment of tension was relieved when one of Coach D's hangers-on, a fat man in a bright orange shirt with a cigar, laughingly waved them on. "That's okay, we're next and I want to hear about the Green Oaks game back in '73."

"Oh, I remember that one…" and Coach D was off again.

The third hole was a short par five with tall grass and then a creek bordering the right side all the way down. Paul played his ball out of the rough on the left, while Frank and Barry walked down the right side of the fairway. They noticed a couple of kids looking for lost golf balls in the tall grass about 30 yards to the right of the green.

"That's probably a good spot to look for balls," Barry said. "Lots of slicers, especially guys trying to reach the green in two."

Frank noticed one of the kids seemed to be very low in the grass, and the other one was on his knees. Funny way to look for balls, he thought. Then the kid on his knees took off his shirt, and lay down on top of the other kid, who Frank now realized was a teenage girl.

"Now that's something you don't see on the golf course every day."

Barry had been watching Paul's shot out of the left rough. "What's that, Frank?"

"A couple of teenagers screwing in the bushes."

"Huh?"

Frank pointed with his nine iron, and Paul walked up to join them, immediately grasping what they were looking at. He just laughed and walked up to the green. Frank and Barry looked at each other before walking up and joining Paul.

On the sixth hole the threesome notice one of the grounds crew taking a nap under a big oak tree, his lawn mower parked nearby. The twelfth hole featured two old timers fishing the big pond that sat to the left of the green. A golf cart that had broken down sat dead in the middle of the thirteenth fairway. When they pulled up to the fifteenth tee they found the foursome there had abandoned their game and were now sitting in their carts pulling beer after beer from a big red Budweiser cooler. The empty cans were strewn around them, and they laughed loudly when one of them, a fat man in plaid shorts, fell out of the cart. Frank, Paul, and Barry ignored them and played through.

The three walked off the eighteenth green without replacing the flagstick, since it was missing.

"Do you want to grab a beer?" Paul said.

"Sure, but not here," Frank said. "How about you, Barry?"

Barry was scanning the driving range, which sat about 50 yards away. "Sure. I'll have a pop."

"Meet you at Harborside," Paul said, citing his favorite bar nearby.

It was late Saturday afternoon, between the crowd watching the 1pm baseball games and the early evening drinking group, so the men had their choice of tables.

"What a sorry excuse for a golf course that place is," Paul said.

"Wait a minute. We forgot to pay," Barry said.

"We did forget to pay," Frank said.

"Good," Paul said, pulling on his beer. "Wasn't worth much, anyway."

"It's sad, too. Because we sure had fun there when we were kids," Frank said. "Remember when we snuck back that night and found the keys in the cart?"

"Man, we drove that thing all over," Barry laughed.

Frank pointed to Paul. "I was sure you were going to drive right into the creek on hole number 14. We were up on two wheels. That was wild."

"That's not the only wild thing that happened on number 14 that summer," Paul smirked.

"Really? You took a girl out to the golf course?"

"Who was it?" Barry asked.

"Sabrina Davis."

"I always liked her," Frank said. "Her brother and I worked together at Jewel Foods."

"Remember when Tommy G caught us playing hockey with our putters on the practice green?" Barry said. "Man, he was mad."

"Tommy G is always mad. Did you see him coming out of the clubhouse today?" Paul said.

"He is a piece of work, that Tommy."

After a few more stories the men headed to the parking lot.

"How's the job hunt going, Frank?" Barry asked.

"Really slow. But I've got an interview Monday."

"Great. Good luck."

"Thanks."

8

May, 2008

"Mr. Jordan? Mr. Horne will see you now."

Frank stood up and followed the administrative assistant at Swinney & Talbot down the narrow corridor and past the trading floor. While most of the people on the floor looked to be in their 20s, his eyes scanned the room and picked out the few workers with a little gray hair, or no hair at all. He needed to see those outliers to keep hope alive, as he knew getting a new job at his age would defy the odds.

This was his third interview since being let go, and it was becoming tiresome to watch the interviewers parse their words so as to avoid any hint of age discrimination. Of course, that was probably why he got the interviews at all – companies trying to prove their open-mindedness by interviewing an older worker.

While he'd dropped the dates off his resume to make it just a bit harder to discern his actual age, the experience section of his resume made it possible to connect the dots. Frank still looked young enough, in good physical shape and with little gray, and with Kate's help he had upgraded his wardrobe enough to pass for maybe 45 or so.

"Hi Frank. Thanks for coming in, Horne stepped around the desk so they could take the chairs around a small table in front of the window. "Can I get you anything? Coffee? Water?"

"No thanks, I'm good.

Horne paused to look over Frank's resume. "You have an impressive body of work." After another pause, "So you were at Bridgestone. Do you know Mike Kennedy?"

"I do. He was covering utilities when I was on telecom and media. Solid analyst."

"He's a member at Oak Lake with me," Horne said, mentioning a mid-level country club. "So why are you here?"

Frank declined to say what he was thinking: "Because I need a job, you idiot." He figured Horne asked the open question to see how Frank would play this: either explain why he was let go at First Fidelity, or what Frank could bring to the table now. He chose the latter.

"I love the markets and have a lot I can offer to Swinney & Talbot. My numbers were good at First Fidelity and I'm looking for a good opportunity to help someone make some money."

Frank detected just a bit of disappointment in Horne at that answer. So he wanted me to spill my guts about First Fidelity, he thought.

"Did you have a lot of client contact at your last position?"

At your last position, Frank thought. Like he didn't know where his last position was. This wasn't going well.

"I did. The guys at Seaport and at Redstone were strong relationships and I help them beat their benchmarks 6 years out of the last 7." Frank referred to a couple of clients that had their money managed by his group at First Fidelity

Horne pulled out a pad of paper and a pen. "Which people there were you close to?"

Frank needed to throw out a little fishing line here. "Before we get into lists, can you tell me a little about the opportunity here?"

Horne thought a minute and put down the pen. His eyes moved to the window. "Swinney & Talbot is a small shop and we're always looking for talent. When I saw your resume I thought it was worthwhile to see if there's a good fit. Right now we have someone covering telecom but that doesn't mean things can't change. Everything's fluid here. We're just looking for good people."

He paused, and Frank assumed he was checking to see if Frank had bought it. He hadn't.

Horne picked up his pen again. "Now which people were you close to at Redstone?"

At this point Frank knew Horne had only called him in to get some information on Redstone, a big hedge fund. The interview was a sham. There was no job here.

Frank figured Horne to be about 40 or 41, so he took a chance that he wouldn't know much about '60s and '70s pop culture.

"I knew their top trader, Al Lewis. Although he had a drinking problem." Al Lewis had played Grampa on the Munsters, and as a vampire he would surely have had a drinking problem. Horne eagerly wrote that down, almost breaking into a smile, and Frank knew he had read the situation correctly.

He continued. "Gary Cheevers is the head trader there, and he plays things very close to the vest." Naturally, as that was the name of an old time Boston Bruin hockey goalie.

At this point Horne was writing as fast as he could, still barely concealing a smile. "Great stuff. Who else?"

"One of the portfolio managers is Anton Dvorak."

Horne paused and looked at Frank. Uh oh. Had he gone too far by invoking the 19th century Czech composer?

"How do you spell that?" Horne asked.

Frank went on just a few more minutes, floating Lisa Luebner (Gilda Radnor's character on Saturday Night Live), Ed Burroughs (author of Tarzan), and Gordon Liddy (of Watergate fame) before thanking Horne for the time and excusing himself. Horne gave him the usual comments at the door: we'll review your qualifications and be in touch, etc. but he couldn't even do that with any sincerity.

Frank walked out the glass atrium to the car.

Now what?

9

Paul rang the bell at Julie's house and just for a second he thought he had forgotten the concert tickets. No, they were in his pocket behind the Nokia cellphone.

The door opened and Julie stepped out wearing jeans that accentuated her long legs and a teal top with drawstrings in front. Paul had been a little smitten with her since the first time they met for coffee, and the way she looked tonight added to that sensation. He had waited until the wiring job at her house had been completed and now he was glad he had done so. It had been uncomfortable enough for him just to finish the two day job, with her walking around the house in those little shorts all day. He hadn't felt like this since high school, and he embraced the feeling.

"You look so handsome," she said, smiling at him as they walked to Paul's van. He realized he should've said something like that to her sooner. "You look fantastic, too," he feebly responded.

They shared concert stories on the drive out to the

Allstate Arena in Rosemont.

"Your favorite concert of all time?" he asked.

"Eagles. 1974 at the Stadium. How about you?"

"Stones. 1975. Also at Chicago Stadium. The stage was this giant five-pointed star, and before the show started the prongs were pointed straight up. Then Mick Jagger climbed up a little ladder to the tip of the front prong and the whole stage slowly opened like a flower, and he rode down towards the audience. Really cool."

"That sounds awesome."

"It was."

"Worst concert ever?"

"Hmmm. I'd say ZZ Top at Poplar Creek. Early 80's. They came on late and about halfway through it just poured. Then the car wouldn't start. So we're totally soaked, and my dad had to drive all the way up to jump the battery. Fortunately it was not a date. Just me, and my friends Frank and Barry."

"Sounds very soggy," she said.

"Your worst?"

"I was at the Riviera when this big fight broke out. Everyone was shoving and I was with my girlfriends and one of them got knocked down pretty hard. Everyone was screaming and the bouncers started throwing people around and these two guys were just slugging each other in the middle of the scrum. I was so scared."

"That does sound bad."

"Hopefully if it happens today I'll have you to protect me," she said.

"At this concert tonight? There won't be any fighting with this crowd," he said.

Ringo's All-Starr band put on a good show, but Paul and Julie headed out before the first encore to beat the traffic out of the parking lot. They were walking down the corridor when Julie pulled back.

"I don't believe it.

"What?" Paul asked, looking around.

"It's my ex-husband. Coming towards us. In the gray shirt."

Paul located the guy she was looking at as he strode toward them with a smirk. He had a black friend with him that looked big, maybe 6'3."

"Julie!" the ex said just a little too loud. "Fancy seeing you here."

"Hi, Gary."

"You look great! Clearly you're keeping up with the gym membership." It didn't sound like a compliment to Paul but was he willing to let Julie call the play.

"You're nice to say that. It's good to see you, Gary," Julie said, and her choice appeared to be to keep moving on.

"Wait a minute." Gary shuffled to the side to block their exit. Not in a provocative way but a clearly unwelcome. Pointing at Paul with his thumb he asked, "Who's your friend?"

Julie sighed, "Gary, just let...."

Paul offered his hand. "I'm Paul. Good concert, huh?"

Gary briefly turned to Paul. "It sucked." Then he focused back on Julie, but said nothing. Paul sized up Gary's friend, who seemed plenty buzzed, judging from his glossy eyes and thin smile.

Julie said, "We have to head out. It was good to see you, Gary."

This time Gary and his friend stepped in front. Paul took Julie's arm and started to move around them.

"Hey, man. Don't be rude," Gary said. "We're just being friendly."

"No problem. We're just in a hurry," Paul said, ushering them past the pair. The crowd in the corridor started to move back into the arena for the encore.

Gary grabbed Julie's arm but spoke to Paul without looking at him. "Don't be an ass. We were married once, you know."

Paul figured they would back down once push came to shove. Now it was time to find out. "Let's finish this discussion in the parking lot," he said.

"Oh, a tough guy. Okay, tough guy. Let's go."

Gary's friend still hadn't said anything yet.

The four walked briskly out the nearest exit, where just a few people were standing, and Julie looked at him.

"Paul, what are you doing?" she said softly.

Paul just shook his head. "Don't worry."

He ushered Julie ahead of him out the door and turned towards the two. It was time to see which way it would go.

Gary squared up on Paul, with his friend to Paul's left. Perfect. This would work just fine.

Gary started to speak, another good sign. "So now what are you…."

Before he could finish Paul swung to his left and landed a short right to the black man's nose. It cracked and blood started to run down between his hands as he raised them to his face.

Before Paul could come back with a left, Gary grabbed Paul's jacket with both hands.

Paul kneed Gary in the groin and grabbed the back of his collar. He hit him with a short left to the mouth, and took a step back to make sure that it was over. It was. Gary was on one knee trying to catch his breath, while his friend was bent over with his back to them holding his face with both hands.

Paul turned quickly and he and Julie took off to the car

at a trot. He kept his head down, only sneaking a couple peeks behind him to make sure they were in the clear. When they reached the van they quickly climbed in and drove out.

Neither spoke for 15 minutes. Paul's hand started to throb, and he was afraid that his brief moment of anger had cost him the relationship. What was he thinking? She's already told him she didn't like fighting. Such a dumb move.

Finally Julie broke the ice.

"I was wrong," she said, confirming Paul's fear that it was over before it really started.

She turned to him and smiled. "This was my favorite concert ever."

10

Paul picked Frank up in his van, despite the abuse he knew that would inspire.

It was the second Friday of the month, which meant book club for Kate and watching the Chicago Cubs game for Frank. They were headed over to Barry's house, as he had become increasingly available during the evenings. Obviously, that didn't reflect well on his relationship with Rachel.

As Frank opened the van door, Paul removed a clipboard and some duct tape from the passenger seat and tossed them into the back. Frank stepped on a pair of pliers as he climbed in.

"Say, I'm glad you stopped by. I was wondering if you had a 6 volt capacitor in here. I need one for the garage," Frank started.

"Do you even know what a capacitor is?" Paul said.

"I know what a flux capacitor is. It allows the DeLorean to go *Back to the Future*."

Paul reached behind him. "I think I have one right here." He reached behind him, pulled out a long screwdriver and poked Frank in the leg.

"Damn!"

"Oh sorry. That was the 8 Volt capacitor. My mistake."

"Who owns this van, you or Candor?" Frank asked.

"I do."

"That explains why there's no signage on it."

"Reduces the odds of a break-in."

"What are they going to steal from in here, nostalgia?"

"Funny."

They pulled up to Barry's house, a red brick colonial with immaculate landscaping. The houses in the development were almost all identical size, with little room between them but decent size back yards without fences. There were few secrets in this neighborhood.

Barry opened the door to greet them, but before he could Rachel yelled from the kitchen, "Did you get enough beer?"

"Yes, I got enough beer," Barry answered in an annoyed tone.

"I'm just asking." Rachel's tone matched Barry's annoyance.

The men moved into the family room to watch the game on Barry's big screen TV, delighting Rex, the hyper active yellow Labrador, who yapped at their feet.

Rachel soon appeared in workout clothes. "Hi, Frank. Hi, Paul. Barry, you forgot to put the food out."

"They just got here. Plus I didn't want to waste the good stuff on them. Do we have the generic chips?"

Rachel ignored him. "How's Kate doing? She still running things at the school? And how's the job hunt going?" Rachel rarely waited for answers, preferring to ask a bunch of questions to feign interest.

"Kate's good. The job thing, not so good."

She turned her sights on Paul. "And you. You probably have a girl in the van waiting for you right now."

Paul shrugged. "Hey, I'm not like that anymore."

"Oh, sure you're not. Barry, don't forget to pick up a cake for tomorrow. And don't get the cheap supermarket kind. Go to the bakery."

"What's the difference?"

"The difference is…." Barry was spared the rant by Rachel's cellphone ringtone. "Hello? Hi, Lois. Just heading out to the club. Hold on." She covered the phone and looked at Barry long enough to demand, "Bakery," and resumed her conversation. "No, it's fine. Nobody." She exited the room without saying goodbye to Frank and Paul, who snuck quick glances at each other.

Barry filled the awkward vacuum. "Who's pitching for the Pirates today?"

"Doc Ellis," Paul offered. Ellis had pitched for the Pirates in the 1970s.

"I thought it was Elroy Face," Frank offered, naming a Pittsburgh pitcher from the '50s and '60s, and the tension of the moment had passed.

Baseball took them back to better days, if only briefly, and that getting that feeling back was increasingly important to them now.

11

Paul was in a very good mood this morning. He'd been out with Julie a few times now, and so far none of the usual deal breakers had emerged. Typically, Paul would gently probe until he inevitably found one, all the while hoping that he wouldn't. Did she have an obsession with cleanliness? Or religion? Or politics? Or animals? Did she have adult or semi-adult children with big problems? Any financial black holes? Criminal record?

While he considered himself pretty much a take-life-as-it-comes type of guy, he was particular about companionship, which probably explained why his best friends were from his childhood. When he thought about it sometimes, he was amazed that anyone over 55 ever found anyone tolerable to companion with. Or was it just him, and he had become too set in his ways?

Anyway, it was different with Julie. He wasn't afraid to find out more about her – he relished it. What was missing was the fear that he'd find the deal breaker. Even if something popped up – and he expected it eventually would – he had no concern about it. This was definitely a new feeling for him, and it explained his sunny disposition as he pulled into the industrial park where Candor Electric had its office.

He grabbed a cup of coffee from the pot on the breakroom counter and wandered into the conference room where the electricians received their job details. It was uncharacteristically empty. Tony Abato saw him out of his office door. "Hey, Paul, hang out there for a few minutes while I finish with Julio."

Tony had run Candor for 20 years, and Paul had been on board for 18 of them. He and Tony weren't friends, but Paul liked his style and he was willing to take a little less money to not have to change jobs. He figured that if he did change jobs, someone at the new shop would probably rub him the wrong way, and life was too short to deal with jerks. Nobody at Candor fit that bill, a tribute to Tony's management.

It took much longer than he expected before Julio finally emerged from Tony's office and walked briskly out the door. "See ya, Paul," he said.

Paul wandered over and knocked on the side of the open office door and Tony motioned him in, cradling the phone in one ear.

"That's right, the 15th is the last day. No, I don't need any more time. I know. Yeah, me, too. You've been a solid guy. Thanks. Okay. Thanks."

Tony hung up and looked at Paul.

Paul sat down and took a sip of coffee. "That didn't sound good, Tony."

"It's not." He took a deep breath. "We're closing."

Paul sat up. "What the hell? We got plenty of business."

Tony shook his head. "Nah. Not really. We've been

47

losing money for about six months now. But that part's okay, I can weather that."

"So what's the problem?" Paul demanded.

"The problem is I took out an adjustable rate loan on the house 3 years ago, and I use that to fund the business, you know, working capital. Now I have to refinance it and because of this damn recession I don't have the equity in the house to make it work anymore."

Tony shook his head. "It's so messed up. The people at the bank are the ones that pushed me into taking out the adjustable loan in the first place. 'Look at how low your payments will be' they said. Yeah, great. Now Wendy and I have to move in with her parents. Sixty-two damn years old and I'm living with my in-laws. Can you believe it?"

Paul sat back to take in the news. And to think this day had started out so well.

Tony continued. "I'm really sorry, Paul. You know how much Candor means to me and you're a big part of everything here. I feel horrible that it got so screwed up."

Paul sighed. "This is really bad, Tony. I don't know what to say."

"No kidding. I haven't slept in 3 weeks. Wendy is hysterical. She's losing her house."

"There's nothing you can do? You have a great business here, someone's gotta be willing to lend you the money?"

"Are you kidding? In this recession? I've been all over, trust me. The banks don't care about a small business like this. No one does."

"Yeah, I hear you. My friend got laid off, too. It's brutal," Paul said. "Listen, Tony, I know you did all that you could. The economy is terrible and everyone's struggling. I get it. It was 18 great years, man."

"I really appreciate that."

Paul stood up, and Tony handed him a work order, his last. He didn't have work for all of his crew but wanted to take care of Paul. He said quietly, "We're in business until Friday. I'll talk to you again before that."

Another Candor electrician, Phil Henry, appeared at the door, unaware of how his life was about to change. "Tony, I saw Julio whip out of the parking lot. What's going on?"

"Give me a minute Phil," Tony said.

When Paul got to the door Tony called after him, "Hey, how's it going with your new lady?"

"Things with Julie are great." Paul chuckled. "One thing's great and now the other thing's crap. What a joke."

"Hey, if you're happy with her that's huge. You can always get another electrician job."

"Sure, at 56. I'll be in big demand."

"You'll be all right."

"If you say so. See ya, Tony." Paul walked past Phil Henry on his way out.

"How you doing, Paul?"

"You'll find out in about 2 minutes, Phil."

12

"Mr. Harrison will see you now."

Frank rose from the lobby chair he'd been waiting in for 45 minutes. If they wanted me at 11:15 why didn't they just schedule it then? he thought, then caught himself and got back into the moment. It wasn't the waiting that bothered him – he certainly had the time – it was the implication that they could make him wait, that he needed something so desperately that he had to wait. His whole life he'd tried to keep from being put in desperate situations, and each time he sat in a lobby waiting to interview now felt like a little piece of failure.

Harrison was short, maybe 5' 7", and fit. Eight by ten photos of him on a racing bike and in running gear stood in the credenza behind his desk. A triathlete, Frank figured.

"Welcome, Frank. I'm glad to have a chance to talk with you. Sorry about the delay."

"That's okay, I'm glad to have the opportunity to talk with you, as well."

They went over Frank's history, with Harrison showing

real interest. Frank thought, this firm is small, maybe after all these years of working at big firms it would be nice to try a smaller one, a good finish to my career. He allowed himself a slice of optimism.

As Harrison started talking about the firm, Black Arrow Management, his visage changed and he took on a serious look. "We do things just a bit differently here, as you may or may not know. As a smaller competitor we like to stay lean and mean, our attitude is more fierce than the others."

Frank adopted a serious look to match Harrison's.

"Your resume is strong, and you seem to have good relations with a lot of great hedge funds especially as well as other money managers. Do you think you can translate that into good business every month?"

"Sure. Those guys know my work and trust me," Frank said, as "fiercely" as he could. He wondered where this was going.

"At Black Arrow we eat what we kill," Harrison continued, "And a guy like you can really do well here." He paused for effect, and seemed to be reading Frank intently.

"Sounds great." But now Frank was really lost.

Harrison leaned back and steepled his hands, the universal symbol of artificial thoughtfulness. It was 30 seconds before he spoke.

"What I'm proposing is bringing you on….."

Finally, Frank thought, the words I've been waiting to hear.

"…on a commission basis," he finished. "Whatever fees we can directly attribute to your work with these hedge funds will go straight into your pocket. Minus the overhead charges, of course. With the relationships you have there's no limit to what you can pull out of this place."

And no bottom, either, Frank thought. He had to tread carefully here, in case there was some other way to make this work.

"So no base salary, just the commissions I generate?" he asked, trying to clarify without revealing his disappointment.

"We don't operate like that here," and with that Harrison launched into how his firm was like the US Marines, that they were gladiators, hunters, gunslingers.

Actually, you're a bunch of nerds imagining yourselves as vicious warriors while you shuffle paper around and play at your computer keyboards like video gamers trying to scrape some commission crumbs off a good idea or two, Frank thought. There was no saving this interview, other than to exit in a memorable way.

"Well, that appeals to me, because my great grandfather was a tribal warlord in Hawaii," Frank said. He stood up raised his right knee up to hip height, paused, then put it down hard. Then he repeated it with his left.

"Abana. Maya Rontowa!" He shouted gibberish.

At first Harrison was unsure of Frank's sincerity, but then seemed to buy into it. He slapped his desk with glee. "That's outstanding! I knew you had that special something we're looking for."

"Tolu. Nocala!"

Harrison kept smiling but now had an uncomfortable look about him.

Frank stepped up to Harrison's desk and slowly bowed. "Magambo."

Then he turned and walked out.

"Wait!" Harrison cried. "Where are you going? I love your spirit!"

Frank kept walking.

13

The following Saturday Frank, Barry, Paul, and Paul's friend Doug walked into the Ravenswood Golf Club and approached the front desk.

"Can I help you gentlemen?" asked the assistant golf pro.

"We have a foursome and would like to play eighteen," Barry said. Frank stood beside him as Paul looked at hats.

"Do you have a reservation?"

"No, we're a walkup."

"I can get you off the tee at 8:36. It'll be $64 each."

"I saw on your website a rate of $42," Barry countered.

"Yes, but that's only available on the internet. I can't give you that rate here."

"But you have an opening at 8:36, right?"

The assistant looked at the computer screen. "Yep. Sure do."

"And if I book it on the internet right now, I can take that slot for $42 each?"

"Uh-huh."

"So what if you give us that rate, and save me the trouble of standing here, getting online with my phone, and booking the 8:36 tee time?"

He looked again at the screen. "Hmmm. I'm not sure how to do that."

"It's okay, don't worry about it." Barry stepped aside for another golfer to pay for greens fees. He took out his phone, signed onto the Ravenswood's website, and in a few minutes was back in front of the desk.

"Hi, we're the 8:36 group. We booked on the internet," he said.

The assistant looked at his computer screen. "Stone? Foursome?"

"That's us."

"That'll be $42 each."

Paul had a 6 foot putt for par on the 5th hole, but hit it too hard and it slid 3 feet past the hole.

"Every time!" he said, and it was true; Paul had no touch around the greens.

"I'll give you that one," Frank said, conceding the putt, as he turned to move on to the 6th tee.

"I'll take it," Paul said, and quickly scooped up his ball. "Good par, Barry."

"Thanks."

Even after his second double bogey in a row Paul's friend Doug kept insisting that he was a much better player than he was showing today.

"I don't understand," he said after yet another errant tee shot. "Usually driving is the best part of my game."

Maybe so, Frank thought, but every one of your drives today has sliced into the far right rough. Every single one. Why do men always profess to be much better golfers on other days than they are on that particular day? And why did Doug care what Frank, Paul, and Barry thought of his golf game anyway?

"I don't know what I'm doing today!" Doug lamented.

I do, thought Barry. You're opening your shoulders at address, not finishing your backswing, and swinging too hard, probably to try to impress three guys that do not care one bit about your game. As usual, Barry was the best player of the group, with a sweet tempo and compact swing.

The other three hit their drives and started down the fairway.

"Any action on the job front, Frank?" Paul ventured.

"Nah. Everyone's cutting, not adding."

Barry asked, "What would you really like to do, Frank?"

"Stop with the New Age stuff, Barry," Paul snapped. "He likes to make money."

"No, it's all right," Frank said. He was thoughtful for a moment. "I still like the markets and I do enjoy researching companies. It's just all the corporate crap that I can't deal with." Frank laughed. "Of course, right now I'd love to be dealing with corporate crap, because it would mean I had a seat at a firm somewhere."

Barry pursued, "I just mean that if the corporate jobs are so hard to find, is there something else that would be satisfying to you?"

"That's a nice thought. I still need to make some money. I mean, the boys are gone and all, but I don't have enough set aside to just play golf every day."

"But would you if you could?"

"I don't know. I do love golf."

"You're eligible for the Senior Tour," Paul cracked.

"I'm 4 over par after five holes," Frank said. "I don't think that's a realistic alternative."

14

Barry noticed Larry Santi's white Corvette in his driveway as he returned home from the course. He started to get that uncomfortable feeling that events were unfolding in a very bad way.

Rachel and Santi were on the patio with large wine glasses and clearly enjoying themselves. It made Barry realize he hadn't seen Rachel joyous like this in a long time. When Rachel saw Barry, her look wasn't one of happy surprise, it was more like he was intruding on her fun.

"Hi, Barry. Larry stopped by."

"So I see. What's up, Larry?"

"I was visiting a buddy of mine who lives around the corner on Pine Street and figured I'd stop by and say hello to you guys. You play South Lake?"

"Ravenswood. Shot 85," Barry said. He wasn't sure if he was supposed to excuse himself and shower, allowing them to continue whatever this was, or pretend to be social and sit down for a drink. Of course, whichever he chose would be criticized by Rachel later. Things had been going that way for a while.

"I'm going to let you guys enjoy your conversation. And your wine." Barry couldn't resist the little jab, before excusing himself to go upstairs.

Larry Santi had always shown just a little too much interest in Rachel, laughing just a bit too hard at her jokes, smiling just a bit too big, and letting his eyes linger just a little too long where they shouldn't linger. Barry doubted that he actually had a friend around the corner on Pine Street. Santi had made a lot of money trading commodities, and wasn't shy about flaunting his wealth. His wife, Debbie, was large and loud, a stark contrast to Rachel, with her dark good looks and Pilates-toned body. Santi himself was bald and soft, and thus a contrast to Barry, who was short in stature but still carried the same 32 inch waist he'd had in college. Rachel clearly enjoyed the attention she received from her old friend.

Barry took his time in the shower, making sure that Santi would have left by the time he finished, then he dried himself off, threw on a tee shirt and shorts, and walked down to the kitchen to grab a snack. He knew what to expect next.

"What was that wine comment about? Do you think I drink too much?" Rachel asked, leaning against the counter with her arms crossed.

"No. I was just surprised to find Larry here and a bottle cracked open on Saturday morning," he said calmly.

"It was almost 1 o'clock, and I was just being a good host to our guest," Rachel countered. "You were gone all morning. So what?"

"Our guest? I think he was your guest."

"Okay, so he was my guest. What's the difference?"

"Fine. Forget it. What did Larry have to say?"

Rachel saw that despite his obvious distain for Larry, Barry was not interested in arguing. He rarely was, preferring to fire a little salvo – like the wine comment – and then retreat to neutral ground. She found that tactic particularly annoying, yet she was grateful he was not the type to engage in a long drawn out shouting match, either. She had seen some of her friends make big public scenes with their husbands – or ex-husbands – and she had no stomach for that. She would have preferred a middle ground to their arguments, but Barry seemed to show little interest in that, so she resigned herself to just move on, as she had so often recently when they had their little flare-ups.

"He's taking Debbie to Paris in August. He was just telling me about their trip and asking if I had any recommendations," Rachel said. Attempting to move on, she asked, "Do you want me to make you a sandwich?"

15

This was the Wall Street job Frank really wanted. All American Asset Management was well-respected both by Wall Street and by other money managers. He had assumed that at 57 he was too old for them to be interested, but his friend Walter Reilly had pulled enough strings to get him an interview, and he was really primed for his shot.

"Mr. Jordan? "Ms. Black is ready for you now." Right on time. This was a tight organization and that fit him just right.

Carly Black came out from behind her desk to greet him. "Hello, Frank. Thanks for coming in."

"Thanks for the opportunity."

They sat at the small table in her corner office on the 46th floor, with a south view featuring Soldier Field. She wore a slate gray dress that showed plenty of tan, taut leg. Her black hair was pulled back, revealing silver earrings which paired with a wide silver necklace and large diamond ring on her right hand. Her wedding ring finger was empty.

"Walter had very nice things to say about you," she said.

"He is also a very big supporter of yours," Frank replied.

Carly stopped and smiled a little too long. Oh, no, Frank thought. Did I say the wrong thing? I was just trying to return a compliment. Did it sound cloying?

"Walter and I worked together at G & T."

Okay, no harm, Frank thought. He realized just how badly he wanted this job.

Carly leaned back and crossed her arms. "What do you think makes you a good analyst, Frank?"

"I would say it's a combination of having the experience of being in the business for 30 years, but still retaining the passion for finding a great company that other analysts have overlooked. I've seen enough to not be taken in by misleading accounting and glib executive road shows, and lived through enough market cycles to know when performance is company-specific as opposed to industry- or market-driven."

Carly's blue eyes were focused on Frank, and a light smile played on her lips.

He kept pitching. "I still love to find a gem among companies that are overlooked because they're too small, or in the wrong industry, or have a history of bad management that has now turned over."

"So you still have that inner fire?"

"Absolutely."

"You still want to dig through financial statements and listen to earnings calls?"

"Absolutely."

Again she held Frank's gaze a few extra seconds, before looking down at his resume. "You played college football? At Wash U.?"

That was thirty-five years ago, Frank thought. "Yes, I did. Linebacker."

She leaned forward, put his resume back down on the table, and smiled. "I love football. I did my undergrad at Yale and never missed a home game. Such a great combination of strength and intelligence, the physical and the mental. Don't you think?"

"No doubt. It challenges both aspects."

"I like that it's not just about strength and speed, but requires a blend of physicality plus intelligence. You know, it's that type of person I find most interesting."

She asked him questions about several of the industries he followed, showing a solid perception of current market trends, and about his work history. She did not ask him about what happened at First Fidelity. He figured either she had the contacts to find out herself, or that she was more focused on the future. Either way, he was glad to not have to cover that experience.

"Frank, I have to say I'm impressed with you. When Walter called I was willing to do him a favor, especially given your, um…"

"Long record of achievement?" Frank helped.

Carly laughed. "Yes. Thanks for helping me out. I don't want to run afoul of HR."

Frank shook his head. "You're safe with me."

"Yes, I can see that," she said. Again, an extra second of gaze, then a smile.

"All American is a great firm, and I really think I can be a real asset to your effort here." Frank felt no reason to pull any punches, and went for the close. "What are your concerns about me?"

Carly leaned forward and placed her interlaced fingers on the table. She looked Frank straight in the eye.

"As I said, Frank. I find you interesting. As a candidate. Let me see about moving things to the next level." With that she stood up, prompting Frank to do likewise.

"I enjoyed meeting you."

"I enjoyed meeting you, as well. I hope we can move forward."

"Me, too, Frank."

16

Barry sat in the conference room wondering if even the extremely thin man who was giving the talk on "Techniques in Inventory Management Controls" was actually interested in the topic. Barry certainly wasn't. He scanned the room at the Conrad & Co. accountants and most of them seemed to be intently following the presentation. In his head, he ran through possible reasons as to why he couldn't muster even a curious interest in the topic:

He could have a junior person do the inventory work for his accounts.

He could have a junior person brief him on the pertinent points after the meeting, and due to Barry's experience and proficiency in accounting (he was very good), he could grasp the concepts in five minutes rather than 45.

He no longer cared that much about his progress at Conrad & Co.

His marriage was in trouble, which trumped everything.

The first two points were a source of pride, as after 30 plus years in the business he'd reached a point where he could take shortcuts without consequence.

The latter two points scared the hell out of him.

After Dean had stripped the Jackson-Hoyt account from him, Barry had sensed an even bigger turn in the tide, and yesterday's events had proved that theory. While Dean could be hotheaded, he had never yelled at Barry, especially in the office. Yet yesterday he had used another late payment from Capitol to berate Barry in front of several other accountants. That was not an accident.

In fact, the more Barry sat in that meeting and thought about things the more he felt moved to do something, to take action, move the needle. He started to feel an inner force that almost had its own will.

He stood up, gathered up his notebook, and walked out of the room. The speaker only hesitated a second before continuing to drone on.

Barry walked back to his office and closed the door. He checked his inner force and yes, it was compelling him forward, pushing him to do something completely out of character.

He sat down at his computer and composed an email.

TO: All employees, Conrad and Co.
FROM: Barry Stone
RE: The future
It has been my pleasure to work at Conrad & Co. for the past 21 years. I have enjoyed working together as a team to build a great organization, and I have great respect for the hardworking employees here. Thank you for making my time here productive and enjoyable. I will miss working with many of you.

I am resigning my position as vice president effective immediately. I wish you success in future endeavors.

Barry read over what he had written, took a deep breath, and hit "send."

17

July, 1969

"Hey! Hey! Holy Mackerel! No doubt about it! The Cubs are on their way!"

Frank, Paul, Barry, and their friend Rick heard the Cubs song the minute they got off the El train at the Addison stop and walked down the stairs to street level. It was a bright summer day in Chicago, they were 18 years old, and the Cubs were in first place! Life could not be better.

They bought grandstand tickets at the window for $2.50 each and entered the park. Organ music was playing as the teams warmed up in the green outfield grass: the Cubs in their white pinstripes with the bright blue and red Cubs insignia over their hearts, and the Mets in their gray flannels with orange and blue trim.

"Who's pitching today? Paul asked.

"Holtzman against Koosman. Battle of the lefties," Barry replied.

Frank led them down the narrow aisle, looking at his ticket and pretending it led him to a nearby box seat. He needed to find the perfect combination of a seating section with some, but not too many fans, and to size up just the right Andy Frain usher. The boys didn't know who Andy Frain was, or if he was even a real person, but ushers in the distinctive blue and gold braid Frain uniforms had been patrolling Wrigley Field since the late 1920's. Some of the older Frains took their job too seriously, and would check their tickets immediately, while others had long lost that desire to enforce the rules and would live and let live. Most of the younger Frains were just college kids on break, and they tended to not care if four teenagers grabbed some empty box seats, but a few were sticklers for the rules, probably trying to look good to move up the Andy Frain ladder, assuming there was such a thing.

They picked a promising section, but were only seated there a few minutes when a younger Frain asked to see their tickets. The four boys all pretended to be confused by the simple section/aisle/seat numbers on their tickets, but they were ousted back up to the higher seating area.

"We'll try again later. Let's walk around," Frank said.

They wandered past their actual section about halfway down the right field line, just taking in the sights. The Little League groups in their matching T-shirts with the adult chaperones. The sun-glassed moms with their kids, all sporting Cubs hats. The city boys with cigarette packs in their T-shirt pockets. Old men hobbling through the aisles with their scorecards and the Sporting News. There were a few longhairs, with dirty jeans and T-shirts advertising their favorite rock band.

And there were girls.

They walked around in pairs, sometimes in small groups. Wearing cutoff jeans and shirts tied in front, with long hair and headbands.

The PA system echoed through the old ballpark. "Attention. Attention please. Have your pencils and

67

scorecards ready. For the correct lineup. For today's ballgame." It was Pat Pieper, the field announcer. He ran through the Mets lineup to mostly indifference.

"And for the Cubs." Wrigley Field erupted in cheers, mostly high-pitched children's voices. "A battery of Holtzman and Hundley. The batting order. 11. Kessinger. Shortstop. 18. Beckert. Second base. 26. Williams. Left Field. 10. Santo. Third base. 14. Banks. First Base. 28. Hickman. Right field. 9. Hundley. Catcher. 29. Young. Center field. And, 30. Holtzman. Pitcher."

Paul got the attention of the peanut vendor. "You got peanuts?"

"Yeah! How many you want?"

Paul and Frank acted disappointed and turned away. "Ah, nah, we want Cracker Jack." They waited until the vendor had turned his back before laughing. "I don't know why that's funny but it just is."

They found seats much better than the ones indicated on their tickets in a section patrolled by a young Andy Frain who didn't seem to care. It was a Tuesday, and the crowd filled in only about two-thirds of the seats. The bleachers, however, were packed.

"That's where we ought to be," Paul said, pointing past the outfield. "They're crazy out there."

"That does look fun," Barry said. "But can you see anything?"

"Who cares?"

The beer vendors carried big buttons on their lapels stating "You must be 21 and prove it," but the boys figured they only needed one vendor who was willing to bend the rules in the name of commerce. They went through five of them before they found the one. "You guys are 21, right?"

"Of course we are."

"You better be."

"Don't sweat it, man."

They nonchalantly placed the beers on the ground by their feet and waited until the vendor had moved up the aisle. Then they toasted each other with the foaming paper cups.

The Cubs scored 4 runs in the 5th inning and Mets manager Gil Hodges trudged out to the mound.

"These guys stink. They're sure to finish last again," offered Rick.

"This is the Cubs year!" Paul enthused. "Who's this coming in to pitch?"

Barry checked his scorecard. "Number 34. Nolan Ryan."

Rick said, "I heard about this guy. He's from Oklahoma."

"Texas," Barry corrected.

"Anyway, he can't find the plate he's so wild. He'll never make it as a major league pitcher," Rick declared.

Frank looked straight ahead at the field while he asked Paul, "So you're really going to go into the Army?"

"Yep."

Frank shook his head. "That's cool, man, but I hope you know what you're doing."

"You know me, I like to go against the grain, ruffle the feathers a little."

"What do your parents say?"

"Well my dad is all for it. Thinks it's great for young guys to toughen up and maybe see a little bit of the world. My mom is scared. She cried when I told them. I hadn't seen her cry in years. In fact, I don't think I'd ever seen my mom cry before."

Barry and Rick were engrossed in another of their arcane baseball arguments.

"No one will ever come close to breaking Ty Cobb's record for hits," Rick stated confidently. "4000 hits? Not a chance, man." Barry replied that he wasn't so sure.

"So when does football start at Wash U.?" Paul asked. "I saw you running the other day."

Frank replied, "I'm running and lifting. Camp starts August 28 and I'll be ready."

Paul turned to Barry. "U. of I., Barry? Don't you want to get away from this state? I mean, half our graduating class is going there. It'll be high school all over again."

"They got a great accounting program there. My Uncle Vic says every business needs accountants. It's a good profession."

"Really? Because no one can count on their own?" Paul joked.

"Shut up."

"Did you hear about that big rock concert in Woodstock? That's not too far from the Wisconsin border," Rick said.

"I didn't hear anything about that, "Frank said.

"Was it on WLS or WCFL?" Paul asked.

"I saw something about it in Chicago Today. It's going to be huge!"

Barry said, "I think it's a different Woodstock, not the one in Illinois."

"What are you talking about?" Rick asked. "Woodstock is near the Wisconsin border."

"I think it's someplace in the East."

Billy Williams sent a ball into the right field bleachers for a solo home run and the crowd stood to roar their approval.

"Slap me five, man!"

"The Cubs are going all the way!"

In the seventh inning, with the Cubs up 6-3, the boys

decided they'd make their way to the bleachers. They walked through the aisle leading to the right field corner and crossed the small catwalk connecting the bleachers to the grandstand. The Andy Frain usher there told them they could enter the bleachers, but not return back to the grandstand.

The late afternoon sun had baked the wood benches, thinning out the crowd, and they settled into a space where they could put their feet up on the row in front. Barry and Rick watched the action on the field, while Paul scanned the crowd, and Frank did some of each.

A girl in cut-off blue jeans and a silver T-shirt seated two rows in front and to the left of the boys caught Paul looking. She smiled and whispered to her friend, who then leaned forward to check out Paul. He smiled and waved. When the girls waved back, he stood up, told his friends, "This is interesting," and went down to sit next to the girls. Paul had always been comfortable around girls, and his friends envied him for it.

Frank's attention was caught by a couple of businessmen in white button-down shirts and thin striped ties ordering another round of beers. He wondered what it was like to work in an office every day, and how these guys could slip out on a Tuesday afternoon to take in a baseball game. It occurred to him that the only people who should be there on a weekday afternoon were students, kids with their moms, and old retired people.

"It looks like Holtzman is tiring. Regan and another guy are warming up in the bullpen," Rick said.

Barry reached over and grabbed his scorecard.

"Number 32. Rich Nye is the lefty."

"Never heard of him."

"He was a starter last year," Barry said. "Not bad, either. But you know Leo, he only likes to pitch 'The

Vulture.'" Barry referred to Cubs' manager Leo Durocher and his penchant for overworking top relief pitcher Phil Regan, who carried the unfortunate nickname of "The Vulture" due to his penchant for swooping in to snatch pitching victories from the starters.

Paul returned from his scouting mission, and the other three played it cool. Barry and Rick kept their eyes on the field, but were listening to Paul intently.

"So?" Frank said.

"So what?" Paul countered.

"So, did you get anywhere?"

"What do you mean?"

"You know what I mean."

Paul enjoyed his status as the bold one. "Well, the one in the silver T-shirt is Jody, and her friend is Karen. They'll be seniors at Woodview."

"That's it?"

"What are you looking for, their measurements?"

"No. I don't know. You were just over there a while."

"I like talking to girls."

By the top of the ninth the crowd consisted of only die-hard fans determined to get their money's worth to the last out, which turned out to be a ground ball to second baseman Glenn Beckert, who threw to Ernie Banks at first to retire Met catcher Jerry Grote. Those who did stay were treated to the spectacle of Ron Santo clicking his heels as he ran down the left field line to the clubhouse door in the corner.

It was a fitting end to the day.

18

May, 2008

Frank's Blackberry rang. It was a business number (ending in 00) that he didn't immediately recognize. "Frank Jordan."

"Hi Frank, it's Carly Black from All American."

"Hello, Carly."

"Frank, I've thought about our meeting and I'd like to schedule another. Are you available on Friday?"

"Friday would be great. What time?" Frank didn't know if he had anything planned but nothing was more important than this opportunity.

"I'd like to meet at 5. They're doing some construction work in the office over the weekend, so we have to be out of there early. I'll meet you at Gibson's on Wabash. It will give us a chance to meet in a more casual setting."

"Great. I'll see you at 5 on Friday at Gibson's on Wabash."

"See you then."

"Thank you."

Beautiful. This could be a great situation. Clearly All American was a firm that cared about performance, but still Carly cared enough about him as a person to want to meet in a casual setting to get to know him. Obviously she didn't care that he was older. Maybe getting cut at First Fidelity would turn out to be a giant blessing in disguise.

19

Julie Adamcyzk was worried.

Since her divorce eight years ago she hadn't really met anyone interesting, and she blamed the 20 pounds she'd gained over the next few years on her general lack of passion for dating. But now, after all those salads, and all that time at the gym, she had finally gotten her shape back, had finally found someone interesting, so the bad vibe she'd felt from Paul's phone call was concerning her.

Part of her wanted to cling to him, try anything to make it work. Just ask him to tell her what it was he needed that she wasn't giving him. She'd change. But deep down she knew that wasn't realistic. She was 47, worked in an insurance office, and while she could finally wear a bathing suit without embarrassment again – a one piece anyway - she was sure Paul could find a younger, fitter companion if he wanted to. Maybe it would be emotionally easier for her to just accept that their relationship, so promising of greater involvement, had simply run its course. She sincerely hoped not.

As she walked out the door of the older office building that housed the State Farm office where she worked, she searched for some kind of relationship Hail Mary pass, something she could do or say that might keep things alive.

"Hi."

Julie was startled out of her thoughts by Paul, who she hadn't noticed leaning on her car just 15 yards away. For just a moment she was excited to see him, but then she remembered the probable reason he was here.

"You surprised me."

"You were deep in thought," he said. "Can I buy you dinner?"

"Sure. Meet you at Harborside?"

"I'll follow you."

Driving over to the restaurant gave Julie an opportunity to prepare herself for the worst, and she hoped Paul wasn't going to be a jerk about the break up. Oh, well. At least he is man enough to show up and do it in person. Some of her friends had recently been dumped electronically.

Paul clearly had something on his mind as they sat down and ordered hamburgers, but she didn't sense he was acting any differently toward her than usual.

"So, how as your day?" she opened cautiously.

"I've had better. I went in to get my work order from Tony and he told me Candor was going out of business."

Can that be what this is about? Julie thought. Did my fears take me way off the reservation?

"You're kidding. Just like that?"

"Just like that," Paul said. "I mean, I had no idea there was anything wrong. Tony said he got stuck in some bad loan, or something and it sank him."

"I'm so sorry," she mustered. "I could tell something was up from your phone call."

"Tony says I'll get paid through Friday but after that

I've got to figure something out." He noticed that Julie's eyes had teared up. "Hey, I liked working there but I'll get another job."

"No, it's not that, "Julie said, more relieved than any other time of her life. "I just had a bad day."

"Oh? Your company went out of business today, too?" Paul joked.

"No, no, it's nothing like that," she said, composing herself. "I just….it's nothing."

He tilted his head at her. "What?"

She shook her head, and wiped her eyes with both hands. "It's nothing. So what are you going to do?"

Paul looked at her a few seconds, trying to figure out what was up, but then moved forward. "I know a couple smaller firms that I can call. I'm gonna try to avoid going back to a big one if I can."

Paul continued on about the relative merits of working as an electrician at a small firm versus a larger one, but Julie paid no attention. She now realized just how much Paul meant to her.

As the waitress cleared their empty red baskets, Julie remembered that she also had news.

"Gary called."

"Really. To apologize?"

"No," she chuckled. "That's not happening. You remember his friend Ron? The one you punched in the face?"

"I punched them both in the face."

"This is serious. Ron says he's going to come after you. He says to tell you to watch your back."

Paul lowered his eyes. "You know the scene in 'Goodfellas' when the law catches up with Ray Liotta?"

"What? No."

"Okay. Ray Liotta's character has been dealing drugs,

77

and at the end of the movie, he's in his car about to pull out of his driveway and take his mule to the airport for another drug run. So the cops come up behind him with the flashing lights and guns drawn and they yell at him and call him names and order him out of the car, and Ray Liotta says, 'Only cops talk like that. If it was wise guys, I never would've heard them coming. I'd be dead.' "

"You think Ron's a wise guy?"

"No. The opposite. The guy you have to worry about is the guy that says nothing and just comes after you. Ron is not that guy."

"How do you know?"

"I just do.

"Paul?"

"Yes?"

"You know we never really talked about that night."

"Uh-huh."

"Were you scared?"

"I haven't been scared since 1970."

She wasn't sure what that meant, but let it go.

20

Frank scanned the restaurant for signs of Carly to no avail. He'd arrived early, as it was, after all, a job interview. He'd struggled with whether to wear a tie, but settled for the classic uniform of gray pants, open collar French blue shirt, and navy blazer. He'd worn his Tag Heuer watch, which he hoped sent the message that he'd been successful in his career, yet he eschewed the more upscale brands like Rolex or Piaget. Frank wanted to be thought of as capable but not flashy. He settled onto a bar stool with a view to the door and ordered a beer to sip while he waited.

A few minutes after 5pm Carly walked in, and strode right over to Frank as if she'd known exactly where to find him. He noticed how much attention she attracted from the mostly male patrons, none of them seemingly embarrassed to follow her every move so closely. She wore a short beige skirt, matching heels, and light knit top which clung, but not in a cheap way. Kate always referred to such a look as "put together."

"Thanks for meeting me here, Frank," Carly shook his

hand and slid onto the bar stool.

"I appreciate the chance to talk again. So you said they're doing work on your office?"

Carly ignored the question and got the bar tender's attention, not a difficult task for her. "You have Stoli? Or maybe Ketel One?"

The bartender nodded, pulled out a vodka bottle and poured.

"So I wanted to get a chance to see you outside the office, in a more informal setting to get to know you better," she said with a smile. "I think sometimes you find out a little more about a person that way." She stopped to thank the bartender for bringing over her drink. "It's important to have the right chemistry."

"That makes sense," Frank said.

They talked about the market for a while, and then Carly brought up Walter Reilly's name. "He gave me my first real opportunity, and sometimes that's hard for a man to do in this business. You know how it is."

Frank told a story about a client dinner where Walter had tried to buy the entire dessert cart. " 'So the waiter goes through all the choices – the New York Cheesecake, the tiramisu, the fresh berries with cream – and Walter says, 'I'll take it.' "Which one, sir?' the waiter asks. 'It. The cart.' Walter says.' The waiter says, 'You can't buy the whole cart,' and Walter says, 'Why not?' and he starts peeling off hundred dollar bills. So they're arguing and pretty soon the manager comes over, and the next thing we know, we're kicked out of there. The client, fortunately, thought it was hilarious. That was a great night."

Carly laughed and put her hand on Frank's. "That's classic Walter. That does sound like a great night."

Frank was taking his cue from her, and when she ordered another round of drinks he guessed things were going well. He took a chance. "Tell me more about your background.

"I grew up outside Boston, and went to Yale. After I got out I started at Bank of Boston for a couple years, then went to University of Virginia to get my MBA. I was with Walter at G & T, as you know, then briefly at Mitchell & Co. before joining All American."

"Are you a runner, or tennis player?" He decided against asking anything more personal. If she wanted to talk about marriages or boyfriends or girlfriends he figured she would. She didn't seem the shy type.

"Swimmer. Actually I swam at Yale. But it's hard to keep that up now with the job. I can't remember the last time I put on a swim suit."

As he knew she had intended, Frank pictured Carly Black slipping into a swimsuit.

"What about you? You look fit," she said.

"I'm kind of a throwback. I still like to just lift free weights. No Pilates, yoga, any of that. I don't know. I just like the simplicity of it. It's just you versus a piece of iron. Either I can lift it or I can't."

Carly reached over and grasped his bicep. "Looks like mostly you can lift it."

They looked at each other for a few seconds, before Carly said, "How do you feel about working under a woman?"

Frank started to feel flush. He really wanted this job.

"I haven't done it before, but I have no issues with that," he said.

"I'm very particular in what I like." She paused, looking directly into his eyes. "Would you have any problem taking direction from me in the middle of the action?"

Frank lowered his head just a bit and returned her

stare. "Not at all."

"I have a good feeling about you, Frank Jordan." Carly reached into her purse and pulled out a hotel key card from the Hyatt Regency hotel across the street. "Why don't you get the check? I'm going to go take a shower." She slid off the bar stool. "Room 406." She turned and walked out of the bar, to the same attention as when she'd arrived an hour ago.

Frank motioned to the bartender for the check and pulled out his phone to text Kate that he'd be home late tonight.

Frank walked in his house about 10:30pm and heard David Letterman's monologue coming from the TV in the den.

"How'd it go with the woman from All American?" Kate asked as he dropped his keys on the kitchen counter.

"It went fine," he said dropping down on the couch beside her. "But I don't think it's going to work."

She turned the sound down with the remote. "Why not? I thought this was the place you wanted to work?"

"I just don't think it's going to work out. Not a good fit."

Kate ignored his vague answer, and knew it was uncharacteristic of Frank. Maybe he would have more to say tomorrow. "Were you there this whole time?"

"No, afterwards I went up to Wrigley to the Cubs game. Just stayed for a few innings." He kept his eyes on the TV.

She turned the sound back up on the TV. Something wasn't quite right.

"I'm sorry about the job, honey," she said.

"Me, too."

21

"You quit my father's firm?" Rachel yelled.

Barry had just walked in from the garage. He walked over to the refrigerator, grabbed a bottle of water, and leaned against the kitchen counter.

"Good news travels fast in the Conrad family."

"Good news? What is wrong with you?"

"I don't know what's wrong with me, but I do know that your father was trying to push me out of the firm. I just beat him to it."

Rachel threw her hands up. "What are you talking about?"

"You know exactly what I'm talking about, Rachel."

"I don't even know you! Do you know how embarrassing this is?"

"Embarrassing for who, Rachel? For you? For your Dad?"

"You're out of a job now! What are you going to do?"

"Don't you mean 'what are WE going to do'? Or am I on my own now?"

Rachel crossed her arms and leaned against the counter. "What does that mean, Barry?"

"It means we're supposed to be a team," he said, pointing back and forth at himself and Rachel. "We. You and me. Not you and your father."

Rachel mimicked his pointing. "WE didn't throw a fit and quit your job. WE didn't do that. You did."

"I knew you would take his side. I knew it."

"How can I take your side? You wake up one morning, go into the job my father gave you, and just quit! How am I supposed to be on your side?"

"Your father didn't give me the job. I had a good career going at Ernst & Young when he asked me to join him," he said. "And I've generated plenty of revenue for the firm. Plenty."

"That doesn't mean you just quit one day! And by email! What were you thinking?" she yelled.

"I was thinking I didn't want to work for a man who supposedly loves my family, and then demotes me! That's what I was thinking."

"Oh, don't be so dramatic. Maybe you're not doing such great work now, maybe he's just looking out for the company," she said.

Barry laughed angrily. "Oh, so now I'm a bad accountant? And it's more important to look out for the company than treat your family right? Are you listening to yourself?"

"Well you didn't have to quit. And not by email. It's so embarrassing."

"Look, Rachel. I know we're having some problems, but I'm not going to work at a place that treats me like that - family or no family."

"Fine, Barry. Go get another job," she said, and turned and went into the bedroom, slamming the door behind her.

That went well, Barry thought.

22

Carly's phone alarm buzzed her awake at 6 the next morning in room 406 at the Hyatt, and she looked over at the empty bed beside her.

She reached over to the nightstand for her glasses, a small concession to being 41 years old, and pulled the phone out of its charging cord to review her messages.

As usual, her schedule was packed with meetings, the most important of which was with the new head of the London office at 9:30am Chicago time. The last guy in that position had been so inept that several key investment bankers had left because of him, and it would take a couple years before they could rebuild that part of the business.

She showered quickly and pulled the suit she had packed the day before out of her bag.

Riding down the elevator she checked the futures markets and saw yet another negative start to the trading day. The financial crisis continued to weigh on asset prices worldwide, which added to her disappointed mood this morning.

She turned right out of the hotel and got in line at a

Starbucks two blocks down. Grabbing the cup with "Harley" scribbled on the side – they never seemed to get her name right - she walked the nine blocks to her office, thinking about last night, and wondering why Frank Jordan had not shown up.

23

June, 2008

Uncle Vic loved the smoked turkey from Sunset Foods, but as Barry started to leave the deli counter, he realized that he had bought the wrong kind.

"I'm sorry, I need the hickory smoked turkey, not the mesquite," he said, handing the package back to the man in the square hat.

"You have to take what I cut, sir. That's the policy."

"I understand that, and it's my mistake, but I'm not going to take this meat."

"Once I cut it and label it you have to take it."

"I get that, but I haven't paid for it yet. There's nothing connecting me to it."

"What do you mean? You ordered it."

"I did, and I made a mistake. But if I give you back the package you can sell it to someone else. Because I'm not going to pay for it."

"You have to take it once I cut and label it."

"Okay. Let's say I take the package, walk around the

store, and place it in the produce section under the rutabagas. There's nothing preventing me from doing that. Do you see my point?"

"You ordered it, I cut it, and I labelled it. You have to take it."

"Okay. You win. Let me also have a pound of the hickory smoked turkey, please."

How do I keep getting drawn in to these inane conversations? he thought.

At some point in the future an unlucky Sunset Foods shopper will pick up a rutabaga and find a pound of mesquite smoked turkey.

Vic Lewis wasn't really Barry's uncle, rather a friend of his father's. After Barry's father had died when Barry was thirteen Vic had been there for him, making sure he had what he needed whether it was the last $500 of college tuition, or encouragement when times were tough. It never bothered Barry that Vic had several other "nephews" that he had helped along the way, rather he considered it an honor to be in that special club.

Uncle Vic was delighted to see Barry, and especially delighted that he had remembered to bring him his favorite lunch.

"You've always been so thoughtful, Barry! That's why you're my favorite nephew. Come. Let's sit and chat."

The phone rang and Vic answered it with a mouthful of sandwich. He listened for a moment, then said, "I'll take care of it. Don't worry. Okay. You, too."

Vic took a deep breath, and looked for something to write on amidst a desk piled high with papers, folders, and envelopes of all size and shape. He grabbed an unopened Commonwealth Edison bill and wrote a note on it. Barry was always very organized, and continually wondered how people like Vic make it through life without missing payment dates, deadlines, and forgetting important events. But Uncle Vic had seemingly navigated his life without major penalty for his lack of order. Anyway, who was he to judge anyone else, with his career and marriage in a tailspin?

"One of my friends passed away last month," Vic sighed. "That was the widow. I've known her since the 1950s." With a quick shake of his head, Vic was back to Barry. And to his hickory smoked turkey sandwich.

"Did you see the Cubs game last night? I hope their pitching holds up."

Major league baseball was the furthest thing from Barry's mind right now. "No, I missed it, Uncle Vic. I've been kind of preoccupied."

Barry unburdened himself with how things had spiraled downward quickly with Dean Conrad, how Rachel had changed, and how he was now living out of the house until things sorted themselves out. Vic listened intently, with the same gentle and understanding eyes that had seen Barry through all sorts of life's trials, both big and small. In hindsight, of course, all of those challenges paled in comparison with what he was going through now.

Even though I'm 57 years old, and Vic isn't going to be able to help me with a check for little league registration, or an internship with an old pal as he did when I was a kid, it's just nice to talk to him and get his perspective, Barry thought.

"As you know, I was married to your Aunt Janet for 55 years. There were ups and downs. You're a grown man, you know how it goes." Vic pointed his finger. "But I think you're right, there's something more going on here. Let me think about this a bit."

For Vic, "thinking about it a bit" meant much more,

and Barry wondered how far Vic's investigation would reach. Like most people, Barry only really wanted to know the truth if it turned out to be good news.

They talked about Barry's career, and his chances of catching on at another firm. Then Vic abruptly changed direction.

"You know, I always thought of you as a great team player, even when you were little. You always saw the whole court, the whole field, knew where everyone should be and how the play should flow. That can help you here. Your team's behind, and you need to change the flow of the game. You need a make a play." Vic leaned forward. "And you will. You'll find a way. I know you have it in you. Don't get too focused on just the ball. This is your moment to see the whole field." Vic winked and sat back.

Barry sat silently for a moment. Although nothing had changed outwardly, he still felt just a little bit better. There was now a tiny seed of something in his thought, a new way of looking at his situation. Yes, he had indeed been viewing circumstances from the microscopic view of where he would live, how he would pay his bills, etc. Vic was right. This was the time to step back mentally, take in the big picture, make his next move with the larger perspective in mind.

The phone rang, but Vic ignored it until the third ring before he answered, still looking at Barry. "Hello?"

Barry gathered himself to leave, anxious for some time alone to contemplate Vic's advice, and he knew just the place. He stopped at the door to wave thanks to Uncle Vic, who covered the mouthpiece.

"Don't be such a stranger. By the way, do you know anyone who wants to buy a golf course?"

Barry chuckled and turned around at the door. "I don't think so, Uncle Vic."

Vic lowered his eyes and looked at him over his glasses. "It's Northcroft."

Barry stopped dead in his tracks.

24

Frank woke up to another day without a job.

The feeling he had wasn't so much a fear that he would never earn a paycheck again. Rather it was the sense that the financial world he knew was continuing on without him, and that each day that he wasn't a participant in it represented a loss of something, although he couldn't quite say exactly what it was. We all have a finite number of days to be productive, he thought, and mine are slipping away.

The way the stock market continued to trade down was also on his mind. His career had spanned an historically strong period of stock gains, albeit interrupted by the Crash of 1987 and the Dot-Com selloff in 2001. For an unemployed man who might have to start pulling cash out of savings to pay his bills, 2008 was shaping up to be an especially scary year.

Kate had been completely supportive of him, which he expected, since she had always been calm and steadfast in the face of adversity. Fortunately, up to this point in their lives there hadn't been much to be concerned about. Their kids had been good students, stayed out of trouble, and been decent athletes. Frank's career had had a nice arc to it, with neither a stratospheric launch, nor a big decline. Until now, that is.

She could tell the job interviews were wearing on him. Oh sure, they'd had a good laugh after the Harrison episode, but now Frank wasn't sure where the next chance would come from. He was 57, ancient for a financial analyst, and the industry was bailing water as fast as it could. That meant more layoffs, not more hiring.

That morning Frank and Kate took a walk along the Lake Michigan shore. He had always appreciated the timeless quality of the Lake – it had been here for thousands of years and would be here long after he was gone. Today it occurred to him that about 200 years ago some Native American brave might've stood right in this very spot, wondering how he would feed his family that fall and winter, just as Frank was doing now. At least the brave didn't have to go on job interviews.

Kate startled him out of his thoughts.

"You just need a special situation. You know lots of people; someone will want just what you bring to the table."

He hugged her. "You're the best. I'm just grateful to have you." He kissed her forehead.

"Do we need to start cutting back? Are there some things that we need to do differently?" He knew it was a question she had wanted to ask for a while, but had patiently held off until now to avoid embarrassing him.

"We're okay. The bonus and the severance will last a while longer. Which is good because I have no idea where to turn next. It's just a disaster out there."

Kate took his arm in hers. "I have confidence in you. You'll figure it out. Maybe it's time to try something new."

Frank laughed. "At my age? You mean be a cowboy?

Or an astronaut?"

"No. I'm serious. Something that you'd really enjoy, even if it didn't pay so well. You know, maybe teach or coach somewhere. You've always talked about that."

He had, in fact, in the back of his mind always fancied the idea of teaching economics at some small college, and maybe coaching a little baseball or football. It was fun to have that prospect out there in an idealized way, especially when the investment business was going bad. But now that that day was actually here, and the prospect real, the idea had lost some of its appeal. Once the dream becomes reality, it loses its luster.

"Maybe," he managed.

"I'm just saying, the kids are gone, and you said yourself we're okay financially. Maybe this is the time to do something for you. I don't know. Is there anything like that you'd like to try?"

They walked along quietly for a bit, before Kate asked again, "Frank?"

"Nothing comes to mind."

25

The 17th green at Lakewood Golf Course was sloped towards the front, making downhill putts very treacherous. Nonetheless, Frank sank an18 footer for his four.

"Good par."

"Thanks."

Frank slid the putter back in the bag and walked to the 18th tee ahead of Paul and Barry. He was sorry that only one more hole remained before he had to confront reality again. He also wasn't sure whether he was sad or glad that his friends had joined him in unemployment. While there was a comfort in communal suffering, there was also something about facing the challenge alone that seemed kind of noble.

Of course, they'd all found themselves in this spot through different avenues. Frank had lost a high paying big corporate gig because of the financial crisis. Paul's firm had gone under because of the crisis' effect on the economy, and Barry had just walked out of the family business before he was either further humiliated or pushed out.

That day at Lakewood the trio had been paired up with a college kid from DePauw University who hit the ball a mile. Small talk on the back nine had revealed that he played fullback there.

"Frank played D3 football at Wash U in St. Louis back in the early '70s. Linebacker," Barry offered.

"Really." the kid showed no interest at all.

"That was a long time ago," Frank added. But it didn't really seem all that long ago. How had he gotten to this point in life so quickly?

They all shook hands after holing out on the 18th, and the three men headed to the clubhouse bar. The Cubs game was on WGN-TV. Afternoon baseball always made Frank painfully aware of how he was not working.

"Well. Here's to us." Barry hoisted his beer. "Drinking beer at 3 o'clock on Thursday."

"Great.Thanks for reminding me," Frank said.

"You close on anything, Frank?" Paul asked.

"Zero. The crisis has everyone cutting, not adding. You?"

"I can catch on with one of the bigger firms but I'm hoping not to. I've done that before and it's bad. The bosses tend to be looking over your shoulder all the time, and a lot of the work they sell is unnecessary." He shook his head. "Makes me feel dirty."

Barry said, "Do they know you're a horrible electrician?"

"Look who's talking, Mr. Accountant. How hard is it to add up some numbers? You have calculators and computers, right?"

Barry came back with, "Remember, white wire to white wire, black wire to black wire."

Frank joined in. "It's the green grounding wire that confuses him."

"Oh, this from the genius financial analyst. 'I think you should buy this company.' Like that's rocket science."

A long Cubs home run drew attention away from the insults. High fives were exchanged all around the bar.

Still staring at the TV, Paul asked, "Things still tough with Rachel?"

Barry snorted. "Tough would be an improvement. I don't know which way is up with her."

"She'll come around," Paul lied.

"Absolutely," Frank lied.

"I don't think so. I think she's got something going."

That put a jolt of seriousness into the conversation. Frank said, "What do you mean?"

"I mean I think she got her dad to kind of push me aside at the firm, and the reason may be she's seeing Larry Santi."

"The fat bald guy? Come on."

"The fat bald RICH guy. I don't know anything for sure. I just get a funky vibe from that situation, you know?"

Frank and Paul nodded politely. Based on what Barry had told them they thought it was entirely possible, even likely, that Dean Conrad would try to push out his son-in-law. The old man clearly did not want to give up control of his company, regardless of who it would hurt, and he would always just assume that Rachel would understand and side with her daddy, even at the expense of her relationship with her husband. But would Rachel actually have an affair? And with a married man? That seemed extreme.

"I moved out." Barry said suddenly. He kept his eyes on the TV screen, not wanting to meet his friends' glances.

"When did this happen?" Frank asked, also politely continuing to watch the game.

"A couple weeks ago."

"Where are you staying?" Paul asked. It was the least important aspect of Barry's problem, but asking it bought

97

them time to digest what was happening.

"The Red Roof Inn on Knollwood Road. It's actually pretty nice."

"Did you join their Frequent Guest Club?" Paul asked. It was the dynamic they'd used to deal with life's problems since they were boys.

Barry picked right up on it. "Three more nights and I get an upgrade to a suite there."

"I hear the suites there have both cold AND hot water," Frank jumped in.

"And continental breakfast," Barry said.

"I can't offer that kind of service, of course, but why don't you move in with me?" Paul offered. "I've got an empty room."

"We have room, too," Frank said. "And that way you won't be crimping Romeo's style." He pointed a thumb at Paul.

"Hey I'm just what he needs. I can set him up with some of Julie's friends from her gym." He turned to Barry. "What kind do you like? Tall? Blond? How about a Pilates instructor?"

"Yes, a tall, blond, Pilates instructor would be great. I'm sure they are looking for a 57 year old short, dark, unemployed accountant."

"Hey, you'd be surprised," Paul replied.

"Wasn't there a Seinfeld episode like that? Where George introduces himself to some girl with that line?" Frank said.

"'Hi, I'm George. I'm unemployed and live at home,' "Barry said.

"That's it!" Paul said. "There you go."

"Seriously, you have to stay with one of us," Frank said.

Barry nodded, and briefly looked at his two friends

before examining the label on his beer bottle. "I really appreciate that. I guess I'll take my chances with Mr. Matchmaker here."

Paul smiled triumphantly at Frank, then turned back to Barry. "I'll prepare your quarters, sir."

After another round they headed out to the parking lot, where Frank knew they'd make fun of his car.

"So, Frank, when you pull up to the unemployment office in your BMW, do they look at you kind of funny?" Paul said.

"He probably parks in the handicap spot," Barry piled on.

"So we can eliminate a career in comedy for the two of you," Frank said. After loading his clubs in the trunk, he added, "We really are lighting the world on fire, aren't we?"

Paul shrugged. "It'll work out. It always does." Then he said to Barry, "Bring your stuff by tonight and I'll get your room ready."

26

He's going to make fun of my Volvo, Barry thought, as he pulled into Paul's driveway.

Paul came out the front door and walked around to the rear of the open hatchback. "Does that car come with children in soccer uniforms, or do you have to buy those separately?"

"I can see why you'd want to know, since you drive a red kidnapper van."

"Hey, that's work related, or at least it was until recently."

"What's inside of your van now, 1975?"

"Hey, that was a good year, 1975. The Bears drafted Walter Payton."

Paul had a three bedroom ranch house, and the front bedroom had been set up for his friend. Although there had been many overnight guests, almost all had been female.

Barry hadn't brought much, two duffle bags of clothes, his computer, five pairs of shoes, his golf clubs, and a box of papers. Like a lot of husbands separating from their wives, he had packed in a hurry. It was an extremely sad chore that was best handled quickly.

As he hung his clothes in the closet he heard Frank come in the front door, and a few minutes later he joined his friends in the living room.

"Am I just in time to avoid helping?" Frank smiled.

"Perfect timing, as always," Paul said as he flipped through the cable channels before settling on ESPN. Sportscenter was running highlights of the previous night's action, and a few minutes into it the familiar sight of Wrigley Field appeared.

"So, where do you guys stand on the job search?" Barry asked, prompting curious glances from Frank and Paul.

"I've got one thing going," Frank replied, but he really didn't.

"I've got a couple leads. Nothing firm yet," Paul added. "You?"

Barry knew he had to present his idea carefully, so he held back his trump card. "Well, I had an interesting idea. Instead of going back to work for someone else, what if the three of us bought a business together?"

There are very few men who don't envision themselves running a successful business. In fact, almost all men spend a good part of their lives thinking about how the companies they work for would be better run if only they were in charge. (Not to mention the government.) But no one perks up at the chance to run their own business like an unemployed man.

"Us three? What kind of business could we run together?"

"A golf course."

It was quiet, as Frank and Paul tried on the idea. Whereas a man with a steady job might quickly dismiss such an idea as impractical, someone searching for a new opportunity would search his mind for ways that it could work, rather than reasons why it couldn't, even if deep down there were serious doubts. Barry let out the fishing line a little more.

"And not just any course…." He paused for effect. "Northcroft! Our old stomping grounds.

"Look, I could do the accounting and computer tasks, Paul can handle maintenance, and Frank, you've been looking at companies both large and small forever. You know what works and what doesn't. What could be more perfect than the three of us running Northcroft?"

"Can we afford a golf course? I don't even know what they cost."

Barry pulled out a sheet of paper where he had broken down the costs and the financing and handed it to them. "It's very doable." He still kept the trump card in his pocket.

Frank and Paul looked at him suspiciously. "So this idea isn't just coming out of left field, is it Barry?"

"Just take a look. See what you think."

Frank, of course, knew how to look at a company's financials better than anyone, and was surprised to see that Barry was correct – it might actually be doable if they could negotiate the right price. Paul did as they expected him to do – pretend to understand what he was reading and to rely on Frank's expertise.

Frank put the paper down and leaned back. "The owners don't seem to be asking for much. That makes me suspicious."

Barry handed Frank a short report prepared by the business broker, still leaving out that Uncle Vic had put him on to the deal. "I was surprised, too. But those are the numbers."

"I've never owned a business before," Paul said. "Might be kinda cool."

Frank continued to examine the pages in front of him. He really wanted to be able to say that they could make it work, but his natural skepticism held him back. "I don't know. It looks good, but ....I just don't know."

"Well, just think about it," Barry said, continuing to let out fishing line. Now just ask me the right question, he thought.

They ordered a pizza and watched the Cardinals-Mets game. At 10, Frank got up and headed for the door. Now's the time, Barry thought.

"So how did you hear about Northcroft being for sale?" Frank asked.

Bingo.

"Oh, Uncle Vic mentioned it to me. He thought it might a good deal for us," Barry said as nonchalantly as he could. He knew Paul and Frank considered Uncle Vic a very shrewd businessman, and if this deal indeed had Vic's stamp of approval on it, his friends would go for it.

"Uncle Vic, huh?" Frank said, equally nonchalantly.

"Yeah, he knows the doctors that own it are having all kinds of problems and they'll be aggressive sellers."

"Interesting," Frank said. "Well, I'll let the Odd Couple go back to the TV."

Paul shut the door. "You didn't mention Uncle Vic was behind the deal," he said to Barry.

"Didn't I? Anyway, think about it."

And with that Barry went off to his room at Paul's house, confident he had landed his fish.

27

Kate loved the penne pasta with pesto and pine nuts at Giuseppe's, while Frank preferred the eggplant parmesan.

After the waiter had taken their usual orders, she leaned forward and looked at him. "So you're really going to buy a golf course with Barry and Paul? Are you through with the financial markets?"

Frank slouched back. "I'm afraid the financial markets are through with me. Firms are looking for younger, cheaper talent – although they can't say that, of course. That is, if there is a firm that's hiring at all. Most are just reducing headcount as fast as they can. This is a bad time on Wall Street."

"It's not too good on our street, either," Kate said.

"No. No, it's not."

"So how are we doing on money? Can we actually afford to buy a golf course?"

"Well, we're okay for a while with the severance package. Not forever, of course."

"But what about the golf course?"

"The golf course is interesting. The down payment is not as bad as I expected, and there's plenty of room for improving operations."

"But it requires a big loan from the bank," Kate said.

"It does. We definitely need to increase revenue to pay that," Frank said.

"And you think you can do that?"

"Uncle Vic thinks we can."

Kate sat back in her chair. "So this is an Uncle Vic production?"

Frank shrugged. "That's really the only reason I'm even thinking about it."

She thought for a moment. "Well, he does have a way with deals."

"Do you hate the idea?"

"No, I don't hate the idea. I just want to make sure you're doing it for the right reasons. I want you to be doing it because it's a good deal, not because...."

"Because I can't get a job on Wall Street?" he completed her thought.

She reached her hands across the table and took his. "You know I always have confidence in you."

"Even to run a golf course?"

Just then Walter Reilly stopped by the table. He leaned down to kiss Kate on the cheek and Frank stood up to shake hands.

"I don't mean to interrupt your dinner. I was on my way to the men's room and saw you guys here," Walter said.

"It's so nice to see you," Kate said. Looking around, she asked about Walter's wife. "Is Lisa here?"

"No, it's actually a business dinner. The guys from Murphy & Carrow are over there. Big drinkers. I can't keep up anymore. Remember those days, Frank?"

"I'm trying not to."

Walter laughed. "Me, too. Say, I talked to Carly, and she said you pulled out of consideration for the job at All American. I would've thought that spot would fit you pretty well."

Frank tensed, and he could feel Kate looking hard at him. "Yeah, they just seemed to have most of my sectors covered well already. But I really appreciate you putting me up for that. I really do."

Walter was too smart to buy that line, and Frank knew it, but he also knew Walter wouldn't press the issue in front of Kate. What Frank didn't know was exactly what Carly had told Walter.

"Of course. If I come up with another idea I'll call you," Walter said. "Kate, so nice to see you again."

"Thanks, Walter. Give my best to Lisa."

"I will. See you guys."

After Walter left, Frank said, "Classic Walter. Always entertaining. The guy just lives the investment business."

"You didn't tell me you pulled out of the All American job. I thought that was the one you wanted," Kate said.

"I thought it was. But I was wrong."

Kate put down her fork and looked at him.

"Let's talk about this at home," he said.

"So she wanted you to come up to her hotel room?"

"Yeah."

"What did you say?"

"Nothing. I just didn't go."

"Where did you go?"

"To the Cubs game. Like I told you."

"But you didn't tell me this beautiful 30 year old woman wanted to have sex with you!" Kate yelled.

"Well, she's more like 40, and nothing happened."

"That's not the point!"

"What is the point?" Now Frank was yelling, too.

"You should've told me!"

"Told you what, that I didn't have sex with somebody?"

Kate closed her eyes and took a deep breath. "You should've told me that a woman tried to get my husband to sleep with her. Is that so hard to understand?"

Frank spread his arms. "I don't know why you are so angry about this. Nothing happened. Nothing happened. There's nothing to tell."

"There is something to tell. My husband has dinner with a woman, who then comes on to him, and he doesn't tell me about it!"

"I thought it was a job interview dinner! I didn't know she was going to come on to me!"

"Why didn't you just tell me about it?" Kate demanded.

"Because nothing happened! Look, next time a woman comes on to me, I'll immediately pull out my Blackberry and let you know."

"Oh, so you're planning a next time?"

"No! I'm just trying to figure out why you're so mad."

"Too late for that." Kate stormed off into the bedroom and slammed the door.

Great, Frank thought.

28

Frank headed out at 6:30 the next morning to the supermarket to buy flowers and croissants. He would've preferred a florist and a bakery, but they didn't open until later and he figured it was better that he had something waiting for Kate when she woke up, thus avoiding that awkward moment the morning after a fight. It wouldn't fix everything, but it was a start.

He had just put the roses in water when Kate came into the kitchen. She spotted the roses and the white wax paper bag. "What's this?"

"Just a small peace offering."

"That's nice of you," she said, but without any emotion.

He walked over to her. "I have never cheated on you and never would."

"You still don't under......

"And....," he interrupted her, raising his index finger. " And...And... And I should've told you about anything like that."

She frowned and hugged him. "I don't want you to think you can buy me off with supermarket flowers and pastries."

"I know."

"At the very least that requires real bakery goods."

29

Julie opened the door of Paul's house to greet Frank.

"Ready for the board meeting?" She smiled.

"Depends if you spell it B-O-A-R-D or B-O-R-E-D," he answered.

"Wow. Kate's a lucky woman, being married to a comic genius."

"It takes a comic genius to work with these clowns," he said, walking over to the kitchen table where Barry was shuffling through a stack of papers. Paul pulled three beers from the refrigerator and sat down.

Julie said, "Well, I'll let you get down to business. Paul, offer them some food or something." She went upstairs.

"You guys want anything?"

"Let's just get going," Barry said.

He handed each of them a more detailed report than the one they had originally seen, with five years of financial records, a comparison of the golf courses in the area, some facts about the golf industry in general, and some financial projections he had prepared. To no one's surprise, it was very thorough and well done.

"So what do you think, Frank?" Paul asked.

"Like most things, it looks good on paper. The tricky part is getting reality to match the projections."

"I used very conservative estimates, Frank. I think we can do better than the numbers," Barry said.

"There's nothing wrong with your work, Barry. In fact, it's really good."

"So, what's the problem?"

Frank put the report on the table and leaned back. "Here's the problem. I don't know if I can ever get another decent job in the financial business. I'm 57, and this is a big chunk of our retirement savings. I don't know anything about running a golf course.
And we're in the middle of a big recession."

"But other than that, you're okay with it?" Paul chuckled.

Barry remained focused on Frank. "What are you not saying, Frank?"

Frank got up and stood by the counter. After a few moments he sighed, and said, "I just hope we're doing this for the right reasons. I mean, it looks like a good business, but I keep asking myself whether I'm doing it because I'm afraid I can't find another job."

"And you think I'm doing it because I'm having a mid-life crisis," Barry said.

"Oh, I get the drift now," Paul said. "You think we're grasping at this because we don't have any choice."

"I don't mean it that way, Paul. I was only talking about myself," Frank said.

"No you weren't. You're talking about all of us." He stood up. "You probably don't think we can raise our share of the money, either."

111

"Don't put words in my mouth. I'm just saying this is a tricky thing."

"I can come up with my third, Frank," Paul said.

Frank ignored him and looked at Barry. "Have you thought this all the way through? I mean, with all that's going on?"

"You mean my marriage?"

Frank was on the defensive now. "Look, I don't know where things stand with you. I mean, you know…"

"You mean financially?" Barry said.

"Yeah. And just everything. I'm just…"

"I can come up with my third, Frank."

"Okay, okay."

The three were silent for a few moments, looking at their beers. Finally, Paul looked at Barry. "This will work, right, Barry?"

"There's never any guarantees in these things…."

Paul threw up his hands. "Oh, great. I thought you were sold on this thing. Now you're backtracking."

"I'm not backtracking. I'm just being careful in my estimations."

"Well that sure sounds like backtracking to me."

"What are you looking for? I'm just saying…"

And at that very moment the answer became clear to Frank. "I'm in."

Paul and Barry looked at him incredulously.

"I'm in," Frank repeated.

"Me, too," Paul said.

"Let's buy a golf course," Barry said.

30

On one side of the conference table sat the three prospective buyers of the club, with their attorney. Frank, Paul, and Barry had hired another of Vic's "nephews," Arthur Brinkman, to represent them.

On the other side of the conference table sat the Highview group, current owners of Northcroft Golf Club, with their attorney, Josh Fine. Dr. Fine (Josh's dad), Dr. Klein, and Dr. Shein were all busy on their cellphones, talking with varying volume.

At the far end of the table sat Vic Lewis.

Arthur was outlining the specifics of the offer. "My clients are bidding the number you see on page 2. The other points that need addressing are listed on page 3, including the valuation of mowing equipment and the pro shop inventory...."

"How do I know what's on the x-ray? I'm in the lawyer's office!" Dr. Klein's agitation with his cellphone conversation caused a brief pause in the negotiations.

Josh Fine responded to Arthur, "Okay, so this offer is

contingent on the bank loan, yes?"

"Shein. S H E I N. No, not like sunshine." Dr. Shein was similarly frustrated by the person on the other end of his phone call.

Arthur continued unfazed by the cacophony. "Yes, but we have a tentative approval letter from the bank citing terms that make this deal work."

Dr. Fine hung up his phone. "What are we talking about, Joshie?"

"Dad, don't call me that here. I told you."

"Ah, my son the Ivy League lawyer." Dr. Fine motioned with his thumb at Josh.

"Dad!"

"Okay. Sorry."

"No, don't do that!" Dr. Klein threw his free hand up in the air. "Are you trying to kill her?"

"No. Get the spelling right." Dr. Shein said loudly and slowly. "Yes, it matters. Because last time I got the incorrect drug shipment and I couldn't treat my patients properly."

"So this is the price your clients will pay, based on the valuations on page 3?" Josh asked.

Dr. Fine's phone rang. "Dr. Fine."

"That's the price," Arthur affirmed.

Frank and Paul tried to shut out the noise and concentrate only on what Josh and Arthur were saying. It wasn't easy to do. Barry snuck a look at Uncle Vic, who sat with a bemused smile.

"Three milagrams! Three! Not 30!" Dr. Klein stood up and started pacing.

"We have a bad connection. Who is this again?" Dr. Fine asked.

"Yes I would like to talk to the general manger," Dr. Shein said. "Put them on."

Josh moved the piece of paper in front of his father and pointed at the number on page 2.

"You're from where?" Dr. Fine asked. He looked at the number Josh pointed to and nodded his assent. "Hello? Are you there?"

Josh got up and pointed out the number on page 2 to Dr. Klein. He also nodded and resumed his conversation. "That's right. You do that," he said into his phone.

Josh then performed the same act with the very animated Dr. Shein, obtaining the same response. He then sat back down and looked at Arthur.

"Gentlemen. We have a deal."

"That was the craziest meeting I've ever seen. And I work on Wall Street," Frank stood in the lobby of the building with Vic and his two partners.

"You used to work on Wall Street," Paul said. "Now you own a golf course."

"They didn't counter our offer," said Barry. "I was surprised. Makes me a little nervous that they know something we don't know."

"They were pretty distracted in there," Frank said. "I'm not sure they even knew what they were agreeing to."

Barry turned to Vic, who was still smiling. "What do you think, Uncle Vic?"

"Oh, you got a good deal all right. And they were distracted."

The three looked at him.

"You staged those phone calls," Frank said.

"Congratulations, boys. Make Northcroft great again."

31

It was pitch black at 4am when the white van pulled into the Northcroft Golf Course parking lot. The driver dropped out of the van and went around the back door to grab his tools. He walked quietly to the front of Northcroft's clubhouse and met up with the men that had hired him.

"Thanks for coming so early, Pat," Paul said. "I really appreciate it."

"Ten free rounds, don't forget."

"I won't forget. And it's five free rounds. " And with that Pat started changing the locks.

By 5:30am only three of the 12 person maintenance staff had assembled, and they were surprised to meet their new boss, Paul Smith. He congratulated them on retaining their job, and explained that only the next five employees that showed up would be as fortunate. Northcroft had become bloated with poor workers, and too many of them, and Paul aimed to trim the fat. After he released them to their assignments, each one started furiously dialing on their cellphones, waking up their sleeping co-workers and exhorting them to get to the course as quickly as they could to save their jobs. Paul's first day in charge of maintenance was off to a good start.

In the pro shop Barry was on the computer systems downloading upgrades and installing new software. He peeled off the dozen or so yellow sticky notes with various reminders of passwords and paths to files and tossed them in the trash. He had, of course, been over every inch of the accounting books covering the past five years and figured it would take about 3 weeks to straighten out the mess.

At 6:45am Frank sat down with golf professional Chris Keller and his assistant pro, Jessica Weaver. Chris leaned forward and drummed his fingers nervously on the table. He had been quite shaken when his key hadn't worked in the door this morning. On the other hand, Jessica was adopting a cooler attitude, sitting back in her chair with arms crossed. Frank closed the door behind him and sat down.

"I can explain about the pro shop money," Chris said anxiously.

Frank shook his head. "You don't need to." The room was silent for a few seconds, then he continued. "Everything starts new today. Going forward everyone's going to do what they are best at, and for you two, that's giving lessons on the range."

Chris and Jessica looked at each other.

"That's right, no more taking tee times over the phone, no more computer entry, no more messing up the merchandise ordering."

"I can explain that, too, you see..." Frank raised his hand to cut Chris off.

"I don't care. Starting today, you guys are strictly giving lessons. Individual lessons, group lessons, demonstrations. We're going to make Northcroft a golf course again, and to do that we need you out on the range. That way you make money, and we make money. Any questions?"

There were no questions, just a relieved look on Chris' face and a satisfied smile on Jessica's. Frank took both as good signs.

Telling Coach D that his services would no longer be required went more smoothly than Frank had anticipated.

"Ah, that's all right," he said. "I was getting tired of telling all those old stories anyway. My wife will appreciate me being around the house more, too. I wish you guys the best in turning the place around."

"Thanks, Coach. I appreciate your understanding."

And with the wave of a big meaty hand, he climbed into his car and drove off.

The only bump in the day was when a foursome of men ignored Frank's instruction to take the cooler of beer out of their golf cart.

"Chill out, man."

"Yeah, we won't bother anybody."

They laughed and drove off.

"Can you believe that guy?" one of them said.

"Who does he think he is?" his companion replied.

They'd had seven beers between them by the time they reached the 2rd green, when one of them noticed two golf carts headed towards them from the clubhouse.

"What the...?" he said, attracting the attention of his pals.

The group was not laughing as four Lake View policeman got out of their carts and arrested them for being drunk and disorderly. The crowd on the driving range cheered as they were driven in handcuffs past the clubhouse in golf carts and loaded into the squad cars.

"We're never playing here again!" one of them yelled as he was led away.

"Exactly!" Frank yelled back.

At 8:30 that evening the last golfer drove out of the lot. Frank sat down on the bench by the 1st tee and tossed his clipboard with the tee time listings to the ground.
A minute later Barry emerged from the clubhouse with three beers, joined by Paul coming out of the maintenance shed. They clinked their bottles together and celebrated Day One of their new lives.

32

Barry woke up at 5:00am and knew he was not going to be able to get back to sleep, not with the meeting with Rachel and the lawyer this morning. He dressed in the dark and snuck out of Paul's house, climbed into the Volvo and slowly turned the key in the ignition, in the universally held belief that doing so would make the engine start in a hushed tone.

When he walked into Starbuck's he was an hour and a half early to meet Rachel, and figured he'd add caffeine to what was already going to be a tense situation. How much worse could it get, he thought.

"If you put $20 on a Starbuck's card and register it online, you get $24 worth of coffee. It's free," said Winona, the smiling barista.

"Well, it's not really free."

"Sure, it is. You buy the card for $20 and get $24 of coffee. Or you can use it for scones or our other bakery goods."

"I have to give you $20 today, right?"

"Yes."

"And then you have my $20 and I no longer have use of it."

"Yes, but…"

"And I don't get $24 of coffee until I register it online." Winona was no longer smiling. "So now, you have my email address, and I'll get constant emails from you every day, offering me the chance to put more money on the card, so then I don't have access to that money either, and I have to delete all those emails. So it's not free at all."

Winona looked at the line forming behind Barry. "Do you want to order something to drink?"

"Tea, please."

He bought a newspaper and settled into a booth at the window. An overwhelming wave of sadness rolled over him.

He thought about how Rachel was a wonderful mother to the boys, extremely patient and always emotionally there for them. Even as teenagers, Derek and Wes had been willing to share their thoughts with her, which Barry knew to be rare for boys that age. At the time, he had been grateful for her devotion to their children, figuring that those times were precious, and that his time alone together with Rachel would come later. Now, as he sat looking out a coffee shop window on a midsummer morning, about to meet with a matrimonial attorney, he figured it was unlikely that time would ever come.

Maybe all the effort she put into the boys was all that she had to give, he thought. Rachel wasn't a bad wife, she just always seemed to have something else to put ahead of Barry. There were many times when he wondered if he was just being selfish, seeking more attention than such a devoted mother had to give. But there had to be more to a marriage than bringing home a good paycheck, coaching the boys sports' teams, and an occasional dinner out alone, didn't there? He also wondered if there had been a turning point, a catalyst that had pushed them apart, or whether it had just been a gradual drift, and a settling of things into their predestined positions.

Then, of course there was the shadow of Dean Conrad. Rachel's almost reverential relationship with him seemed to seep into every phase of their lives. Even after all the years of Barry's employment at Dean's company there had remained that sense of discomfort between them, almost a competition for Rachel's affection. Barry had always seen Dean as egotistical, controlling, and unwilling to let go of Rachel (or her sisters) – but that was an opinion he knew was best kept to himself. Rightly or wrongly, whenever there was friction in their marriage, Barry always saw the invisible hand of his father-in-law.

Barry noticed a pretty blond woman, about 50, enter the Starbuck's wearing a black suit and carrying a large purse plus a laptop bag. He watched as she walked to the counter and got a large coffee to go. Barry realized he was still staring at her when she turned to exit, and she noticed him in the corner. She smiled at him, catching him by surprise, before she pushed through the door to leave.

That was the first time in almost 30 years that he realized he might actually have to start dating again.

From his window seat Barry watched Rachel park the Toyota Land Cruiser and walk into the office building across the street. She looks sad, he thought, and that stirred feelings not of guilt, but of sadness in him, as well. While the frosty tone she had maintained during their recent phone conversations gave him little hope for a quick reconciliation, he truly had no interest in seeing her unhappy. After all, they'd been together 29 years and raised two children. Whatever the future for them held, either together or, more likely, apart, that history could not be erased.

He tossed his newspaper and cup and headed over to join her.

The meeting at Elliott Holcombe and Karasik was an attempt to avoid acrimony – and expense. Barry and Rachel hadn't yet decided to divorce, they just wanted to figure out some ground rules regarding finances, and see what the consequences were if they did go down that path. Barry had no animosity toward Rachel, and while she revealed none towards him either, her businesslike demeanor in the meeting chilled him just a bit. After an hour of discussing what money each would have access to, and what the next step off the cliff would be if they decided to go that route, they thanked Charles Elliott and walked silently to the elevator. They both looked straight ahead.

"Do you want me to wait for the next one?" Barry asked.

Rachel shook her head. "No reason for that."

Great, Barry thought. No reason for that because there's no feelings there?

"There's a Starbuck's across the street. Can I buy you a coffee?" Barry asked.

"Sure," she replied curtly.

At the counter Rachel ran into her friend Corby, and chatted for a few minutes longer than necessary as Barry stood by waiting silently for their orders. The shop was much busier now than it had been when Barry was there earlier, but they found a small table near the door and sat down. It was a tight fit, and they realized they hadn't been this physically close to each other in quite a while.

Rachel said, "The city came by last week. They said we

have to take down the tree by the driveway. It's all rotted, and they're afraid it will fall on the Foley's house."

"That would be okay if the Foleys are in it at the time." Barry thought their neighbors were a little too loud. Rachel ignored the comment.

"I'll call the tree guy on Monday, she said.

"Good plan."

"Wes is in line for a really nice bonus this year after he negotiated that big settlement in the hospital case. I think he wants to buy a new car."

"That's great. I don't know why he needs a new car, but it's his money."

"You think he should save it, right?"

"What's wrong with saving? Once the stock market turns around it will be a good buying opportunity. He can buy a really nice car, then."

"He doesn't like driving that old Nissan. He's a young man, he needs a stylish car."

"Maybe he should buy a white Corvette," Barry said.

Rachel crossed her arms and smiled. "So now we're going to go there, huh? Hey, you're the one who walked out."

"Yeah, after you made it clear you didn't want me around."

"I never said that."

"Oh, come on, Rachel. You did nothing but criticize and get on my case about everything. Your old friend Larry Santi starts coming around again – when I'm not home, of course – and then your daddy starts pushing me out of the firm."

"My father has nothing to do with this."

"Your father has everything to do with this. Twenty-nine years and it's like you never left his house." They weren't shouting, but their tone had other people glancing over at their table.

"Barry, what my father does at the job is just business. It's not personal."

"I'm his son-in-law, and the father of his grandsons. There isn't anything more personal than that. I'm not another employee. I'm flesh and blood. How can you not see that?"

Rachel gathered her bag and phone, stood up and threw her bag over her shoulder. "This is going nowhere. I'll talk to you later."

As she walked out, Barry noticed she hadn't defended her visits from Santi.

33

To clear out the unsold merchandise in the pro shop the new management at Northcroft held a Midnight Madness Sale, with everything – everything - half off. After the last few golfers left the course at about 8:30 one evening, Frank, Barry, and Paul sat around watching the Cubs game until 10pm, and then prepared for the sale. They expected a few early birds, but when they walked outside at eleven-thirty there were 85 people standing in line waiting for the sale to start. The doors opened at exactly 12 midnight, and by 1:30am the pro shop resembled a looting site. They had three cash registers going, and a rent-a-cop positioned at the door, just to remind the customers to conduct themselves properly.

Naturally the good golf balls were the first to go, and the 2 box per customer maximum was very disappointing to the scavengers who had hoped to make a score by posting the discounted Titleist ProV1 balls on eBay. Putting the golf balls on sale wasn't necessary to move them, but it was a sure way to generate traffic. The gloves were next to sell out– maximum purchase 4 pairs per customer – followed by the golf bags and shoes. Lots of stores and websites discounted shirts, but once a shopping frenzy starts everyone wants to add to their collection, especially since most of the golfers didn't have one with the Northcroft logo. Due to the decline in the course's reputation, no one had felt the need to pay full price to display that logo.

By setting the discount at a simple 50% it was easy for the happy shoppers to do the math, which also added to the frenzy. Who wants to take the time to figure out what a 40% discount on a $69 shirt is? Much easier to say, "Hey, $35 for a new golf shirt with a logo I don't have!"

At 2am the three owners sent the rent-a-cop home, rested for an hour, then started opening the boxes of new clothes, clubs, balls, and shoes that Barry had ordered and stacked in back. By 6am the transformation was complete, and the Northcroft Golf Club pro shop had gone from tired to sharp, while the men had gone from sharp to tired.

34

July, 2008

As Julie Adamcyzk rode one of the health club's eight stationary bikes pointed at the TV, an ESPN feature on the Pittsburgh Steelers brought back memories of childhood.

She had grown up in Pittsburgh with two older brothers, Tim and Ken, and like most girls in that family situation she had been rugged and athletic while growing up. Back in the '80s the opportunities for girls to develop those abilities had been limited, and all the opportunities that her daughter Sandra had had sometimes gave Julie just a tiny feeling of resentment. Not resentful of Sandra, of course, but at the timing of her life. In fact she thought a lot about life's timing these days.

She had met Gary, her ex-husband, during her last semester at University of Pittsburgh, when she was feeling insecure about going out into the business world, and he provided an excuse to take a job as an office administrator, rather than the sales job with Dow Chemical that her family encouraged had her to take. Four years older than her, Gary seemed so much more polished than all the guys she knew, and it was easy to fall into an orbit around him, rather than to become her own planet.

Within three quick years she married, had Sandra, and moved to Chicago when Gary took a job at Motorola. She certainly had no regrets about that period of motherhood – taking Sandra to dance classes, basketball, track meets, and music lessons had been fulfilling – but Julie did feel that she had been swept up into a current of a life not of her choosing. She sometimes wondered whether she had really ever made a life choice, or that the timing of things had always made those choices for her.

The worst timing had been when Gary split immediately after Sandra had gone off to college at University of Colorado. Suddenly money was tight, and Gary offered little help, despite what the attorneys had promised. Julie was propelled by events back into the workforce without much of a support net, either financially or emotionally, and those first few years were a real struggle. When Sandra came home from college on break she wanted to be her own person, and Julie's general unhappiness caused a lot of friction between them. She chalked that up to bad timing, too, but now that both of them had matured they shared a wonderful relationship, even though Sandra was miles away in Denver. Julie had thought about moving there hundreds of times, but she never quite seemed to get it done. Maybe she was again waiting for events to take their course.

On the health club TV she watched as a young Terry Bradshaw threw the touchdown pass to John Stallworth in Super Bowl IVX again, Art Rooney hoist the Lombardi trophy, and the feature on the Steelers segue into another Sportscenter show. Julie got off the bike and headed to the locker room. As she pulled the door open she noticed the Honeywell thermostat on the wall. For the last couple of weeks all of those stupid electronic controls now reminded her of Paul Smith, and she hoped his arrival was finally good timing.

35

Frank worked hard to book group outings at the course, often undercutting the competitors' prices to get exposure for the changes at Northcroft. Some of the outings raised the course's media profile, like Law Enforcement and Military Day, where every golfer playing in uniform received half off on their greens fee. They ended up with representatives from 14 area police forces, sheriffs from 3 counties in Illinois and 1 in Wisconsin, and golfers wearing Navy, Army, Air Force, and Marine uniforms. A foursome from the Coast Guard had to cancel at the last minute due to a boating accident in Lake Michigan. Frank struggled to organize a big team picture of all the golfers, with the photographer from the local paper having to climb the clubhouse roof to get the wide angle shot.

The foursomes went off in order, but Frank noticed one of the Navy groups set to tee off at 10:15 still hadn't arrived just 5 minutes before then. He was just about to skip their time slot when a big blue helicopter appeared out of the south, circled the clubhouse, and landed in the 1st fairway about 40 yards from the tee. Out jumped 4 seamen in uniform with their drivers in hand and their golf bags over their shoulder. They ran to the tee to raucous cheers and barely waited for the helicopter to take off before hitting their drives. Despite the excitement of the spectacle, only one drive found the fairway. The video shot from someone's phone went viral, generating some national buzz for Northcroft. One US Marine could be heard to say, "Those damn Navy guys. We should've thought of that." Turning to Frank, he added, "Wait until you see what we come up with next year!"

36

Tony Abato opened up the doors to Candor Electric for what he assumed would be the last time. It may be just some space in a mid-grade industrial park, but it's much more to me, he thought.

He had treated his employees, especially Paul Smith, very well. He knew Paul was a bit of a player, and he had looked the other way at Paul's romantic exploits when other bosses might not have. Fortunately, it had never rebounded back to hurt the business. In truth, Candor probably had gotten a little bit of extra business because of it.

Tony had helped Julio out when some of his family had had immigration issues. He had pushed Oscar to go back to college, and when he hadn't quite cut it at Southern Illinois, Tony had taken him back. Other than one old lady in Glenmoor who couldn't be satisfied no matter what Candor did, his reputation with customers was outstanding. Maybe he should've sent Paul out to "see what he could do" with that Glenmoor matron.

He noticed the headlights of a big SUV pull up outside the door. Looking at his watch, he saw it was almost 9 o'clock, and he'd been there for over three hours putting pictures and trophies in boxes. He was knee deep in old job invoices when a large black man let himself in.

"I'm looking for Paul Smith."

"He's not here," Tony said warily.

The man smiled. "So I see. Can you tell me where I can find him?"

"I'm not sure. You are…?"

"I just have a little piece of business with him."

Tony did not like where this was going. Was this guy a jealous husband? Boyfriend? Tony didn't think Paul had any habits that would bring anyone more dangerous around. He wasn't a cop - a law enforcement official would've flashed his badge already. Tony's eyes wandered for a weapon he could use in case things went the wrong way. The crow bar in the corner was too far away if this man was serious.

"What kind of business, if I may ask?" Tony stalled.

"There's a debt that needs to be paid. He works here, you must have his address."

"You can see what a mess everything is. Leave me your number and I'll find it."

The man reached into his coat pocket. "Let's see if we can speed things up."

Tony froze. He was going to have to give Paul up and hope for the best. The industrial park was empty. No help was coming.

The man pulled out a stack of hundred dollar bills, and counted out 10. He took three steps forward and placed them onto Tony's desk. "I'm just looking for an address, man."

They looked at each other for a moment. Finally, the man said, "Well?"

Tony waded through the boxes towards the desk. He

was closer to the crow bar but that would not help if the stranger had a gun.

"I don't know you, and you don't know me. I'm not giving Paul up for a grand." Tony felt emboldened by the fact that nothing bad had happened yet.

The man smiled. "So you do have an address." He peeled off five more Franklins and added them to the pile. "Where can I find Paul Smith?"

Tony looked at the $1500 in cash on his desk. That money would really help right now, as he wound down the business. Plus the bank wouldn't know about it, and neither would the IRS. If this guy was really dangerous, Tony thought, I'd be bleeding right now. He could give out the address and then call Paul to warn him. What was the harm?

"I'll write it down for you."

Tony took a Candor Electric card, wrote Paul's address on the back, and handed him the card. The man looked at it, then back at Tony with a less friendly glare. "This is Paul Smith's current address, right, Anthony Abato?"

Tony was now grateful he hadn't tried to scam the stranger. "That's it."

The man eyed Tony a few more seconds, then turned to leave. He stopped at the door. "Small business going under?"

Tony sat down. "Adjustable bank loan. Seemed like a good idea at the time."

The man nodded. "Yeah, I know a little bit about loans that go bad." He opened the door and looked back at Tony. "Oh, and don't call Paul and tell him about me. I want to surprise him."

37

Frank walked into Lake View city hall.

"Can I help you?" asked the woman behind the counter.

"Yes, I was wondering if I need some sort of permit to host a concert," Frank said.

"What kind of concert?"

"Well, basically a rock concert."

"On city property?"

"No, actually it would be held on private property, on Northcroft Golf Course, specifically."

"And I'm assuming you have their permission?"

"Yes, I do."

"They gave you permission to host a concert?" She looked at him skeptically.

"There's a new management team there. They're willing to try new things."

She didn't appear convinced, but bent down to pull out a form and a pen. "It's going to be $100 for the permit."

"Okay," Frank said.

"Date of event?"

"A week from Saturday."

"Time?"

"Let's say, 9pm to midnight."

The woman looked up. "The ordinance says the music has to end by 11pm."

"Okay. Let's say 8pm to 11," Frank said.

"Expected attendance?"

"About half a million."

She gave him a disgusted look.

"Just kidding. About 300."

"Does this event have any sort of name?" she asked.

"Woodcroft."

"Are you ready to rock?!" Frank yelled into the microphone.

"Yes!" the crowd yelled back.

"Welcome to Woodcroft!"

The crowd roared its approval.

Frank introduced a local garage band, and then jumped off the wood stage they'd constructed on the 9th fairway. They'd ended up with closer to 400 people, a mix of all ages, and everyone was having a good time. Rainbow tie-dyed T-shirts had been printed up, with "Woodcroft," the date, and a big peace sign on the front, with Northcroft's address, website, and phone number on the back. All three hundred shirts had been quickly given away.

The first band played their set, and then were followed by a hip-hop artist from Forest County Junior College. The final act was an oldies band made of 50-somethings that worked at a downtown insurance company.

Despite Frank's best efforts as emcee, when the final chorus of "Twist and Shout" ended, the night had run well past the 11pm curfew dictated by the city permit. The next day, a policeman showed up at the course with a noise complaint from one of the older neighbors, and Frank promised to handle it promptly.

On Monday morning Frank rang the doorbell.

When the door opened, he said, "Mrs. McCauley? I'm from Northcroft Golf Course, and I'm here to apologize for the noise on Saturday night."

"That music kept me up past midnight," she said.

"Yes, I am very, very sorry about that."

"When you live near a golf course you expect it to be quiet. That's the whole point."

"Yes, ma'am. You're absolutely right," he said. "Is there some way to make it up to you?"

"Like what?"

"Um, I don't know. Do you play golf?"

"No, I don't."

Frank wasn't sure what to say next, and Mrs. McCauley must have felt sorry for him, because she held open the door. "Would you like to come in?"

"Yes, thank you," Frank said.

"Have a seat." She motioned to an old upholstered chair. "I'll get us some lemonade."

The house was decorated as if it were the 1940s, with thick curtains, dark furniture, and two credenzas holding china and other knickknacks. He noticed a yellowed baseball on one of the shelves, and got up to take a look.

"That's a home run ball from Billy Williams." Mrs. McCauley said as she returned from the kitchen with two glasses of lemonade. Frank went over to take one from her and waited until she sat down to do the same. "He was my husband's favorite player."

"Yes, he was a great one. Hall of Fame," Frank said. Was your husband a big baseball fan?"

"Oh my, yes. We used to go all the time," Mrs. McCauley said, clearly warming to the subject. "I remember going to Wrigley Field back in…"

Thanks goodness for baseball, Frank thought, and for the next hour Mrs. McCauley regaled him with sixty years of Cubs' memories.

"Thanks again for the lemonade, Mrs. McCauley," he said as he stood on her porch. "And again, sorry about the noise."

"Thank you for coming by to apologize, Frank," she said.

"I hate to bring this up, but, well, this Saturday we're holding another event."

"Oh?"

"No, no, it's not a concert. We're trying to generate interest in the course, and we thought it might be a fun idea to host an old fashioned movie night. You know, like the old drive-in theaters. We'll sit on blankets and lawn chairs. Oh and we'll be done by 11 o'clock, I promise you that."

"I see," she said. "And what movie are you showing?"

"It's a golf movie, a comedy. It's called *Caddyshack*."

Mrs. McCauley frowned. "Is that the one with Rodney Dangerfield and Ted Knight?"

"Yes, that's the one," a surprised Frank said.

"I love that movie. I'll be there," Mrs. McCauley said.

38

Victor Lewis was born on Chicago's south side to Polish immigrants, one of many that shared the journey through poor but caring neighborhoods in the 1920s and '30s, to hard-won jobs in Chicago's Loop in '40s and '50s, and on through to the green northern suburbs in the '60s. For some, a three bedroom ranch with a detached garage and small yard to mow with a push mower, plus the promise of a better life for their children, was the gold at the end of the rainbow. Others, like Vic, parlayed their shrewd cunning to far greater riches.

Vic and his brother Marvin started a small company making batteries, correctly figuring that the baby boom would require lots of toys, and toys would require lots of batteries. Selling a depleting – but necessary – item meant lots of repeat purchases, and the business thrived for a decade. But the brothers also foresaw that such simple manufacturing businesses would, in time, be replaced by foreigners with cheaper labor, so they sold the battery business to a larger competitor in 1968.

Intellectual capital could not be replaced so easily, and Vic and Marvin opened an insurance agency. People always needed insurance, and the brothers got paid on renewals year after year. The business thrived, and Vic bought a big brick house in Highmoor, where many other successful South Side natives had moved.

Vic Lewis always seemed a step ahead in life, but there are some things that you can't outrun. Marvin died suddenly of a heart attack, and Vic's only child – a daughter, Suzanna – also died of what would become known as Sudden Infant Death Syndrome, but back then was only attributed to tragedy. Vic and his wife Janet did what they'd always done – they persevered through it, but neither of them was ever really the same after that. Helping some of the neighborhood kids like Barry eased some of their pain. After Janet died in 2003 – Vic sometimes joked that the Cubs collapse in the playoffs were responsible – he sold the big house to move into a condo near Lake Michigan. Every Saturday morning, even on the coldest winter day, Vic walked along the shore, talking in his head with Janet.

Vic was on the phone when Barry entered his office with the bag of sandwiches from Sunset Foods, and he signaled him to one of the chairs in front of his desk.

"I'll send you the inscription by email tomorrow. That's right. How long before it's installed? That long, huh? Can you do it any faster? I would really appreciate if it could get done before it gets cold. Anything you can do would be much appreciated. That would be great. You've been very helpful. Thanks a lot. Bye." He hung up and said to Barry, "I'm getting a bench down at the beach dedicated to Janet. Now I just have to figure out what to say on the plaque."

He made a note on a piece of paper already full of them. "You brought lunch?"

"Yep, corned beef on rye, just like you like," Barry said, handing him the hickory smoked turkey on wheat bread.

"Wise guy," Vic said. "How's the Northcroft project going?"

"Well, we're making progress. Bookings are up, but some of that is just the novelty of some of the new things we're trying. Eventually we'll run out of fun ideas and have to provide just a great golfing experience. I hope we can do that."

"Why is that so hard?"

"The merchandising in the pro shop – that we can handle. The general operation of the business end – that we can handle."

"So what's the problem?"

"The problem is the course itself. You know the doctors left it in pretty bad shape. We don't know anything about reviving a golf course, the seeding, the watering…"

"You think my brother Marvin and I knew anything about batteries when we started?" Vic said. "You learn. You're smart. You'll figure it out."

"Maybe, but we have to do it pretty quick."

"You've always been such a worrier. Just keep working hard and you'll get it."

They talked about the Cubs while they finished their lunch, and then Barry approached the topic they'd avoided.

"So, what did you find out about Rachel?"

Vic placed his arms on the desk and leaned forward. "Barry, you're strong, you're going to be able to move past this."

Barry nodded and looked down. Hard work was not going to fix this.

39

Paul and Julie were snuggled on his couch watching Jay Leno when his cellphone rang. She grabbed the remote and muted the TV.

"It's Tony," he said to Julie, opening his Nokia flip phone. "What's up?"

Tony related the visit of the mysterious man, apologizing for giving up his friend.

"You know the jam I'm in, with the bank loan, and all. Fifteen hundred goes a long way, man. I'm really sorry."

Paul was disappointed in his friend, but in his usual way he took the news in stride. He wanted Tony to know he understood his predicament, but didn't want to let him off the hook completely.

"I get it. Thanks for the warning."

"I'm sorry, man. I called you right away. Just be careful. It may be nothing."

If you thought it was nothing you wouldn't have called, Paul thought. If it was nothing, the guy wouldn't have come up with the $1500. Paul hung up.

"What did Tony want?"

Paul ignored the question. "Did you talk to your ex-husband again after he called following the concert?"

"I told you about that. That Ron was mad at you."

"I mean after that. Any conversation?"

"No. Why do you ask that?"

"Just curious."

Julie grabbed the remote, clicked the TV off, and faced him. "What?" she demanded.

Paul told her about Tony's call, the black man looking for him, and whether it had anything to do with the incident with Ron and Gary.

"That night you said you haven't been scared since 1970. What did that mean?"

"You really want to hear that story?" he asked.

"I didn't even know there was a story, Paul," she said. "Yes, of course I want to hear that story."

"Okay," Paul said, turning to face her on the couch. He related being chased by the Viet Cong soldiers through the field that day as a nineteen year old kid. "Here I was, thousands of miles from home, and these guys I didn't even know were trying their damnest to kill me. Hundreds of them. With AK-47s. Shooting at me. I mean, I would've been lying dead in a crappy little field somewhere that nobody cares about. It would've been over. And I just barely made that chopper. If that machine gunner had been a poor shot, or high on weed, or just didn't care, I would've been dead. Dead. After that day, something just changed in me. What could ever be as terrifying as that? Nothing. So it's not that things never bother me – they do. But I can't say anything really scares me. Not after that."

"That explains a lot," Julie said.

"Like what?"

"Like why it doesn't seem like your divorce was as traumatic as mine was."

144

"Well it wasn't life or death, like the other thing was," Paul said. He was quiet for a few moments. Then he said, "We were too young when Abby and I got married. Actually, I was too young. I think she figured I'd straighten out at some point, but eventually she just got tired of waiting. I can't blame her. I was a jerk back then."

Julie held her breath as she silently waited for Paul to continue, not wanting to do anything to intrude upon the moment. Paul was generally fun to be around, but those rare times when he really opened up like this were precious to her.

"I think when my daughter Kristen was born, Abby saw that as my chance to grow up, and it made a difference, but not enough to make it work. We stuck together for as long as we could for Kristen's sake, you know, but by a certain point nothing I said or did was going to be good enough. It just wasn't going to work out."

"When was the last time you talked to her?" Julie asked.

"Abby? She doesn't want to talk to me, and I don't want to talk to her."

"No, not Abby, Kristen. When was the last time you spoke to your daughter?"

"Oh, well, it's been a while," Paul said. "Let's see, we split up when she was eight, and Abby moved up to Wisconsin to be closer to her family. I think the last time I saw Kristen was when I showed up at her high school graduation. Abby was really pissed off about that but I didn't care, I wanted to at least be there for that. So that was the last time I saw Kristen. I called her a few times when she was at college, but it was just awkward."

Julie hugged him tighter. "What do you mean?"

"You know how these things go. When the dad's not around, the mother is always telling the kid what a jerk he is. Everything that's wrong in their lives is his fault. That's all the kid hears. Didn't you do the same thing with Sandra?"

"Yeah, I guess I did."

"It's just the way it is. And to be honest, I deserved it. I wasn't there for here. She has every right to not want me around."

"I get it," Julie said. "It's just so sad. You're not that person anymore."

"You go through life and you make mistakes. You can't go back in time. You do the best you can going forward," he said. "I do hope that someday I can have some kind of relationship with Kristen. I really do."

"I hope so, too. And I'm glad you made it out of Viet Nam alive."

He chuckled. "I'm glad I made it, too. Otherwise I wouldn't be here with you right now."

She kissed him. "I love you."

"I love you, too."

40

Barry figured that with a job at a golf course he now had no excuses for not getting his handicap down into the low single digits. So he scheduled a lesson with assistant pro Jessica Weaver.

As he walked out to the driving range to meet her, she had just finished her lesson with Mrs. Wolliver, who must've been 95 years old.

"That's impressive, trying to improve your golf game at her age. Don't you think?" Jessica asked.

"For sure," Barry said. "Exactly what type of things do you tell someone like that?"

"I make sure she takes the club all the way back to the top with a full shoulder turn. You know, a lot of golfers over 90 years old shorten their backswing and that really hurts their distance."

Barry just looked at her.

"I'm kidding," she said.

Barry smiled. "Thank goodness. The course doesn't need any medical claims."

Jessica moved right along. "So, are you warmed up?"

"It will just take me a few minutes."

"Okay. When you're ready let's hit a few 7 irons and let's see where we are."

Barry tended to be nervous in general, and having to suddenly hit golf shots in front of this beautiful young woman with the great golf swing kicked his self consciousness into high gear. He tried to channel Paul and his unfazed approach to everything in life. Then he focused on the 25 things you have to do right to hit a golf ball correctly.

The first shot was fat, travelling straight but far short of where it should've travelled. Damn, he thought. I'm better than that. He caught the next shot thin – the classic golf swing overcompensation – and it skidded left about 80 yards. Relax, he thought, it's only a lesson. You're not at The Masters. He stroked the next shot better but left it a little right.

"Okay," Jessica started. "You're doing some good things with the swing. Let's try hitting a couple balls at three-quarter speed."

Barry took a deep breath and took his stance. The ball was stroked cleanly but again hung right. Same with the next 2 shots.

"Much better. I'd say you're still swinging at more like 85 or 90 per cent, though. Try to really swing at just three-quarter speed."

He slowed down a little too much and chunked it. "I tend to overcompensate."

"That's typical of successful people. They're used to refining their actions to achieve a specific target."

Barry knew deep down how foolish it was to feel good about something a 34 year old golf pro said after seeing him hit a handful of shots. Yet the comment still buoyed him.

They worked for 45 minutes on his iron game, then hit a few drivers that finally left him tired and sweating.

"Let's end on a good one," Jessica said, and he hit a long drive with just a bit of a tail on it. "Good."

Barry pulled out his wallet to pay her, and added an extra $20. "I'd like to schedule another lesson soon."

Jessica smiled. "To keep the momentum?"

"Exactly."

"Well you know where to find me."

41

While Frank manned the grill in his backyard, Kate and Julie brainstormed which of their single friends would be good for Barry. He sat listening to them in a state of excitement and dread.

"How do you feel about redheads? My friend Marilyn is a corporate executive and really smart," Kate said. "But she might be too tall for you."

"What is she, six-three, six-four?" Barry said.

"No. Maybe five-ten, five-eleven. She's pretty. Very driven."

"Sounds like a great match for a five-nine unemployed guy."

"You're not unemployed. You're a big golf course owner."

"If you say so."

"You know, my friend Veronica just got divorced," Kate said.

"Betty's friend? From the Archie comics?"

"Do you want help or not?"

"I'm sorry," Barry said. "This is hard for me."

"How do you feel about someone really into fitness, but a little younger?" Julie asked.

"Wow. Sounds horrible. Is she rich, too?"

"No, she works at the health club. Her name is Jackie and she's really sweet. I'll ask her if she's interested."

Paul had been keeping Frank company at the grill, but he now wandered over to the three, catching the drift of the conversation. "Tell her that Barry likes her, but not LIKE likes her."

"We're helping your friend," Julie said. "He wants nice girls, and since you don't know any..."

"Ouch."

"Maybe you'd like my friend Carol," Kate said. "She's really nice and her husband died about a year ago."

"What's the rule on that?" Barry asked.

"Trust me, she's ready."

Frank brought the chicken and hamburgers over to the table and Kate and Julie went into the house to get plates.

"What am I getting into?" Barry asked Paul.

"I don't know. But I want details."

Two days later Barry stood outside the door of the Charhouse , wearing the blue jeans, loafers, and Tommy Bahama shirt that Julie had picked out for him. He was looking for Kate's friend Marilyn, advertised as pretty, smart, and nice. And tall.

She's pretty, smart, nice, and successful, Barry thought, yet single and willing to go on a blind date. Oh, well, I guess I'm hoping that applies to me, as well.

Marilyn got out of her gray BMW 3series and walked up to Barry. If he hadn't been on his cellphone checking the Cubs score, he would've noticed that she wore white pants, a navy blouse and sandals.

"Are you Barry?"

Barry looked up. "Oh, yes. I'm sorry." He quickly put the phone in his pocket. "You're Marilyn. Nice to meet you."

They went in and were seated in a booth. "Have you been here before?" He asked.

"I have. I like this place."

"So you work at Chemix," he prompted.

"I manage the marketing. We have eight offices in North America and four in Europe. We have 67 people in the department, and did $896 million in sales last year."

"That's a big number."

"We have 4500 employees worldwide, divided into 3 divisions: consumer, industrial, and government..." Marilyn's phone rang. "Excuse me for a moment. Hello. Yes I received the package. No, it's fine. No problem. Okay. Talk to you later."

"Sorry about that," Marilyn said.

"No, I appreciate the vote of confidence. Thank you," Barry said.

"Thank you? For what?"

"That was your bailout call. Apparently, you don't want to be rescued."

Marilyn blushed and tried to deny it. "No, that was just a friend of mine. I needed to pick something up for her."

Barry picked up the menu. "I see."

"Anyway, we do business in 23 countries..."

As he sat looking at Marilyn his mind started to wander. She was pretty, but not a dark beauty like Rachel. At 57 years old was he supposed to care about that? He certainly cared about it back in 1977, and had married the most beautiful woman he had ever been around. And was it

152

really over with Rachel? It sure seemed like it was, but so far he hadn't done anything that would prevent a reconciliation. Wait, would Marilyn expect him to have sex with him tonight? Was that the way it worked now?

"Barry?"

He had missed her question. "Sorry?"

"Do you have any children?"

"Oh, yes. Sorry. Derek is an attorney in New York and Wes is an attorney in Los Angeles."

"Great. My oldest son works in New York for Citicorp. My middle one is here working for a tech startup, and my youngest, Karen, is in DC working for Senator Karl. Last year she was part of a team that worked on the bill that..."

Barry had always been overly sensitive about people who talked incessantly about their stuff – their job, their family, their house – and Marilyn looked to be firmly in that category. Okay, so he'd gone on his first date since the Disco Era and it hadn't quite worked out. It was a step in the right direction. Now he had to figure out how to disengage gracefully. When he refocused on what Marilyn was saying, she was still talking about her daughter's work in Washington.

After dinner, they stood outside the restaurant.

"So, Barry, time is valuable to me. Are you going to call me? Please be honest," Marilyn said.

Barry hadn't expected to be put on the spot. His initial thought was to evade the issue, avoid any unpleasantness, but something inside him pushed him the other way. He actually surprised himself when he said, "You are very successful and bright, but I'm not sure we're right for each other."

Just as she wasn't good at covering up being caught with the rescue call, she wasn't good at covering up her disappointment at his answer. But she persevered in business mode anyway. "Okay. What makes you think that?"

"The conversation was mostly about your stuff. You hardly asked me anything about myself."

She shrugged her shoulders. "I just figured you were quiet. I mean, if you wanted to say something why didn't you just say it?"

"No, that's fair, I guess…"

"Listen, I'm proud of what I've accomplished. I don't see the need to pretend I'm not," Marilyn said.

"No, you should be. You've got plenty…" Barry started to ease his way to his car. Marilyn seemed to be following him.

"When I started out, no one gave me anything…"

Barry was now actually walking sideways to his car. Running would be rude, right?

"Maybe I come on a little strong, but it's who I am."

Barry opened his car door.

"It was wonderful to meet you, Marilyn," he said, jumping in. He closed the door, started the car, and backed out of the parking space. When he checked the rear view mirror he saw Marilyn standing on the sidewalk with her hands on her hips.

Welcome to the dating world, Barry thought to himself.

The next night Barry met Jackie, Julie's friend from the health club, for drinks at a club she suggested called Victor's. She was running late, but he didn't mind as it gave him time to observe the scene.

Victor's had a well-deserved reputation as a hangout for divorcees, and Barry attracted attention the second he

154

walked in. The women were definitely well put together, and dressed to accentuate their better features. Tight tops highlighted big boobs - some real - all further enhanced by Victoria's Secret artistry. Short skirts revealed tanned legs firmed up by personal trainers or yoga. Sparkling jewelry drew attention to fingers, wrists, and necklines. These women knew exactly which colors and fabrics worked for them, with haircuts to set off their faces just so. Barry thought the faces had a hard look to them, not necessarily angry, but certainly without innocence. It was no wonder Victor's was often referred to as "Victims."

Then there were the shoes. Heels, shiny heels, sharp heels. These were serious shoes. Regardless of the wearer's size, shape, or style, they all wore the shoes. Stiletto heels were the go-to - the confidence shoe – convincing the wearers that the extra height lengthened their legs and give them a hint of power. They were mostly correct.

Jackie, coming from her job at the health club, had changed into the shoes, and in her little black skirt and a short top that revealed just a flash of flat stomach, she also attracted a lot of attention from her competitors as she made her way over to Barry and took the empty stool next to him.

"You must be Barry. Julie said you be wearing a white shirt. Sorry I'm late."

"No problem. What can I get you?"

"Just a little white wine, please." Barry signaled to the waitress.

"How long have you worked at Julie's gym?" he asked.

"Just a couple years."

"It probably allows you to keep in great shape."

"Everyone thinks that. But it's hard teaching classes and doing personal training. At the end of the day I'm wasted."

"I can understand that."

She reached over and touched Barry's arm. "So tell me about yourself. Do you work out?"

"Well, I've had more free time recently, so I probably should do more."

"Julie told me you were going through a difficult time. Working out is a great way to get your mind off your problems. You should come by the club. I'll get you a guest pass and we can see where you are," she said.

"You mean how much I can bench press? I was never much at lifting weights."

"No, we can do some circuit training. I can set up a whole routine for you."

"You really are passionate about fitness, aren't you?" Barry said.

Jackie smiled. "I guess I'm a passionate person in general."

They talked for almost 2 hours. Since he had grown up in the area, and had compounded that by attending the University of Illinois just down the highway, Barry had always felt a little self-conscious about how unexciting his story was. He admired people – especially women – who had a more interesting tale to tell.

"I grew up in Buffalo, or a suburb of Buffalo, called Dunkirk, New York. It's right on Lake Erie,' she said. "I went to Skidmore College, in Saratoga Springs. Ever hear of it?"

"I have. I knew a guy from high school who went there. Played baseball. How did you get from there to here?"

"That's a good question. After college I moved to New York City and worked for the Yankees, if you can believe that. In the public relations department."

"Oh, no, you were part of the evil empire," Barry said.

Jackie smiled. "Absolutely. And proud of it. Twenty-six world championships."

"Did you meet George Steinbrenner?"

"Sure, he was around all the time. I can't speak for anyone else but he always treated me nicely."

What a surprise, George Steinbreener was nice to a hot young woman, Barry thought.

"Do you like baseball?" Jackie asked. "Let me guess, you're a Cub fan."

"I am a diehard Cub fan. And this is our year!"

"Well, they won the division last year and are looking good again this year, so maybe so," she said. "That would be perfect – the hundred year anniversary of the last World Series title."

"You really know your baseball," he said. "So how did you come to be a fitness trainer out here?"

"I met my husband, - my ex-husband - in New York. He was a real estate attorney and did some work for Mr. Steinbrenner. So we went out for a while and got married in 1988. He actually proposed to me on the big scoreboard at Yankee Stadium."

"Seriously? That's fantastic," Barry said. "I've never met anyone who did that."

"It was fun. I'm not sure what would've happened if I'd turned him down…" she laughed. "Anyway, a few years later he got an offer to move to the San Francisco office. This would have been in 1997. I was all excited to move out to California – you know, get away from the winters – and then at the last minute they changed their mind and said they needed him in Chicago. I was not happy. But it was a good opportunity for him so we packed up and came here. I got started working out at the club when the kids were little, and when they got to high school I asked if they had any openings and they did. I've been there ever since."

They ordered another round of drinks.

"Tell me about your kids," Barry said.

"My oldest daughter Hannah will be a senior at Deer Lake High School, and a big soccer player. Last year the girls' varsity team won the sectionals, and she scored one of the goals."

"Yeah, Deer Lake has always had a great soccer program."

"Her sister Dawn plays, too, and she's the goalie. She'll be a sophomore."

"And the ex?"

Jackie took a deep breath and exhaled. "The ex decided one day that he needed a change. He quit law, told me he needed to be free, and he moved to Oregon to be a kayaking instructor."

"Wow. That certainly is a change," Barry said. "I'm sorry."

"It was years ago. I'm over it."

Right now it was hard for Barry to imagine ever being over Rachel.

He filled in the blanks on his life, leaving out the part about Rachel's possible infidelity. "We just grew apart, like they say in the movies," he told her, but he doubted she believed him; there was usually another reason. Still, discretion was important to him, and people working at health clubs come into contact with a lot of people.

Downing all those drinks in that sexually charged atmosphere started to affect Barry, and it occurred to him that this might be the first night he has sex with a woman other than Rachel in 29 years. That thought sobered him up just a bit, and started to make him nervous. If that was where this was headed, he needed to do some quick planning despite the buzz he had on.

He didn't really want to bring her back to Paul's, and he didn't know how to ask if her kids – fifteen and seventeen – were at her place. He could spring for a hotel, but that seemed a little cheesy, even if it was a nice one. Maybe we could find a quiet spot and do it in his Volvo, he thought. Like teenagers.

"You seem distracted," Jackie said. "Is something wrong?"

"No, no. I'm sorry. I don't usually drink this much."

"Maybe you need some fresh air. Why don't you come over to my place for some coffee?"

"Sure."

She grabbed her purse and slid off the barstool. "Great. Why don't you follow me?"

Now he really had to focus. She had invited him to follow her to her townhouse, so sex was probably in play, but not certain. He just didn't know whether it was for coffee and to meet her teenage daughters, or if the kids were out and they had the place to themselves. He was ready for the first eventuality, he had to prepare himself for the second.

He followed her Toyota Camry to a nice group of townhouses in Deer Lake and found parking across the street while she waited for him at the door. When he walked up the sidewalk she unlocked the door and went in. The lights were off, and the buzz in his head started to spread to other parts.

"Have a seat on the couch. I'll get us some wine," Jackie said.

So much for coffee and meeting the kids, Barry thought. It was on.

He sat on the leather couch and looked over the townhouse. The furnishings were a little dark for his taste, with plenty of photos of the girls in various soccer uniforms. The place could've used a little cleaning, but that's probably not a big priority of a working single mom, he thought.

Jackie returned with the wine glasses and sat down facing Barry at the end of the couch. "What should we drink to?" she asked.

"I don't know. New friends?"

"How about to, say, happy endings?"

In Barry's mind he saw a blow torch being lit.

"To happy enters...endings," he stumbled.

Jackie laughed and put her hand up to her mouth to keep the wine from coming out. "Wow. Freudian slip!"

"Endings. Happy. Endings."

"Maybe it will be both," she said. She put her wine glass down, pulled up her skirt, and straddled him. He had to lean into her to put his glass on the table, and there was no turning back.

They only kissed for a few minutes before she stood up and took him by the hand down the hall to the bedroom.

This is happening, he thought. Am I cheating? No, we're separated. Plus I'm 57 years old, I'm not a kid anymore. Plus I think Rachel is sleeping with Larry Santi. Plus it doesn't matter; I'm in too deep now. The die is cast. Here goes.

She kissed him much harder than he expected, but of course his only reference for the last two decades was his wife. And Jackie's body was much more responsive than Rachel's, and he realized he was looking for signals that he was used to getting, and but weren't forthcoming. He'd have to improvise and hope that he found the right path. And boy, she was firm. Any other man would love to trade places with him right now, he thought, but I'm just trying to get from point A to point B without incident.

In the end, he considered it a triumph of will, rather than a stylish victory. It left him physically satisfied, but mentally he felt like he had done something wrong but had gotten away with it.

After 15 minutes of lying together and looking at the ceiling he said, "I don't want to be a jerk, but believe it or not I really do need to be up at the crack of dawn tomorrow. Things start early at the golf course."

"It's okay," she said. "I'll walk you out."

At the door he turned towards her and she kissed him. "Bye," she said, and closed the door.

Barry stood there for a moment. Huh, he thought. We probably don't have a future together, but that was a little abrupt. He started walking to the car. I just had sex with the fittest 45 year old woman I've ever seen – so what if it was just a one-time thing? he thought.

At that point he realized that he had always lived his life for the long term, and maybe a little living-in-the-now would be a welcome change.

Barry's cellphone rang as he drove home from Jackie's townhouse.

"Hello?"

"So how'd it go with Marilyn last night?" Kate asked.

"It went okay. She's, um, a little intense," he said.

"She is definitely a little intense. But she's smart, and very accomplished."

"Yes, she mentioned that. More than a few times, actually."

"You're not just looking for a bimbo, are you, Barry?" Kate said.

"No, of course not."

"Because I don't think that's really who you are."

Barry wasn't sure how to respond to that.

"So it didn't work out with Marilyn," she continued. "That's okay."

"Kate, I really appreciate what you're doing, but maybe we just hold off for now. You know, I've got my hands full at the course."

"Oh, Barry. Don't be silly," Kate said. "You can't give up after only one date. I've got other friends for you."

That's what I'm afraid of, Barry thought.

Julie greeted him at the door. "How'd it go with Jackie?"

"You, too?" Barry asked.

"What do you mean by that?"

"I just got off the phone with Kate, asking me about how it went with her friend Marilyn." Barry slid past her and sat down on the couch. Julie followed but remained standing.

"That's between you and Kate. My concern is my friend Jackie. Did you have a good time?" she asked.

"It was fine. We had drinks at Victor's and…"

"Victor's? That must have been quite a scene."

"Oh, it was quite a scene. Not really a world I'm accustomed to," he said.

"No, I imagine not. So did you like her?"

"She's very attractive. I mean very. And she's nice. It was fun."

"You don't sound too excited, Barry."

"I know. I know. It's nothing to do with Jackie or Marilyn, or anyone," he said. "Everything is just changing so fast for me. I'm just not sure what I'm doing."

"I understand," she said. "I remember when my marriage was breaking up. It's a tough time. If Jackie asks me, what should I tell her?"

"Tell her I think she's beautiful and I'm probably not what she's looking for," Barry said.

Oh, and ask her what I did wrong in bed, he thought.

42

Frank's daughter Lauren launched a social media campaign that aroused interest among the high school and Gen X golfers in the area. She worked in Cleveland for an advertising firm, Sutcliffe & Brennan, and knew how to reach a younger audience. By the end of the second week, the course's Facebook page had over 1200 friends and climbing. The millennials were not the best demographic segment for golf in general, but for Northcroft it was important to demonstrate the course was under new, forward-thinking management. Plus, as more Baby Boomers were logging on to Facebook in an effort to stay current (and to try to spy on their children) it gave the 40- and 50-somethings something familiar to "like" and "follow."

Lauren also used Groupon to attract traffic, and fortunately Barry had upgraded the antiquated computer systems so they were able to handle the increased business.

On Saturdays Jessica, wearing tight black spandex shorts, was positioned on the 510 yard par five 3rd tee, and for $10 a golfer could try to outdrive her. A longer drive than hers that landed in the fairway earned a $75 gift certificate to the pro shop. Lots of the men could power a golf ball farther than Jessica could, just not under the pressure, while keeping it in the fairway. Thus far, there had been only 6 winners. Jessica was allowed to keep the losers' money.

One Tuesday, golfers playing on All-You-Can-Eat Day found their green fees included hot dogs (4rd hole), chicken kabobs (8th hole), pulled pork sandwiches (12th hole), and fried catfish (16th hole). That was a good day for the cart girls driving around the course selling beverages. Not surprisingly, they also did a brisk business in Pepto-Bismol.

Some of the group outings at Northcroft included a custom touch.
For the American Dental Association – Chicago Region outing, members of the maintenance crew were posted at the last four holes on the course, where no holes had yet been drilled into the green. After all dentists in a foursome hit their approach shots to the green, the golfers could then direct the worker to drill the hole at the most beneficial spot for the group.

When the Mystery Writers Guild golfers got to the 5th hole, a 175 yard par three, and looked to aim for the flagstick, it was nowhere in sight. A wooden stake with an envelope attached had been driven into the tee box. The curious players opened the envelope to find the message, "What do you say to illicit a response through the mail?"
"Send me a letter?"

"Write me?"

"Write back?"

"That's it! Right back. The pin is on the right side in the back part of the green!"

It didn't matter much anyway – only three of the 20 golfers hit the green at all. Riddles at the other par 3 holes produced similar results.

The first group of the United Parcel Service outing featured their better golfers, but when they teed off on Northcroft's 14th hole, a 415 yard par four with a narrow fairway, a pond on the right, and trees on the left, one of their drives plunked into the water. As the errant golfer walked up to the edge of the pond to play his next shot, assistant greenskeeper Jimmy Boyle emerged out of hiding in the trees in a golf cart made up to look like a brown UPS truck to deliver a brand new ball to him. Jimmy made 8 more such deliveries to the group of 36 golfers, and even the golfers incurring the penalty strokes had to appreciate that touch.

When the Airline Pilots Union booked an outing, Paul suggested that right before their scheduled tee off time Frank should tell them there's a delay, and make them wait around for an hour or so. Frank thought about it, but passed.

43

"What I want you to do is swing the club without a ball, and let it fly out of your hands," Jessica said.

"Just toss it out on the driving range?" Barry asked. "Just out there?"

"Yes."

"And what about all the people hitting balls along here?"

"Don't worry about that."

"Don't worry about that, you say. My five iron will be lying out there 25 yards away."

"I don't really think you can throw it 25 yards," she said. "But if you could that would be great."

Barry took a deep breath and took his stance. "Okay. You're the teacher." He swung, letting go of the club late. It flew a few feet up in the air and came down about 5 yards ahead. Jessica walked over and picked it up.

"Let's try again, but really release the club. Let it go," she said.

Barry swung again, sailed the club out into the range, and looked at Jessica.

"Much better," she said. Stepping out into the range, she shouted, "Everyone hold up for a second!" The golfers stopped hitting balls and looked at her. She looked at Barry and pointed her head at his club.

He paused a second, then, to relieve the awkwardness of the moment, he made a quick wave of his hand and ran out to pick up his club. "Thank you," he waved again.

Barry was not pleased when he returned to his station. "What was that all about?" he demanded quietly.

"It was about you really releasing your hands at the end of the swing. It was about you not being embarrassed to make a mistake."

Barry was still a little ticked off at the method, but he'd always tried to be an obedient student. His game had definitely been improving since he'd started lessons from Jessica (this was his third). He supposed a little foolishness on the range was okay. He pulled a ball into position and took his stance.

"Plus it was kinda funny seeing you run out there like that," she said, smiling.

44

The moonlight was bright enough to clearly outline the dark figure sneaking past the fence on the far end of the course, near the sixth tee box. He avoided the automatic sprinklers coming on the 12th fairway, which ran parallel to the 6th hole, and noticed how weak the spray was. As he continued in towards the clubhouse, he had to shift the heft of the toolbox to his left hand, and then back to the right a few times. I must be getting old, he thought.

As he approached the sixteenth green he dropped to the ground as headlights swung around the parking lot about 75 yards away from him. Probably just the police making the rounds, he figured. He waited, and sure enough the arc of the lights continued around the lot and was replaced by the red glow of taillights.

He got up, looked around, and pursued his mission.

45

August, 2008

Head golf pro Chris Keller was put in charge of a renewed junior golf effort, and it became so popular that a special car drop off/pickup area for moms had to be designated in the parking lot. The kids loved being able to whale away at the yellow range balls, and the moms appreciated their kids spending time outdoors with their friends while learning a sport. All those little golf clubs and bags were a nice money-maker for the pro shop, too. Sundays were designated as Family Days, and after 3pm a family of up to six members could play 9 holes for a total of only $30.

One day Chris was talking to a group of 10 year old boys when one of them raised his hand.

"Yes, Timmy?"

"My dad says you want to get birdies on the golf course."

The pro chuckled. "Well, that's right. But that's not easy."

"I'll bet I can do it," Timmy said.

"Really? I hope you're right. Anyway, boys, today we're going to work on our putting…"

"Can I try?" Timmy asked.

"Can you try? Try what?" Chris said.

"Getting birdies."

"Sure, Timmy. You can try to get some birdies. Now, let's…"

Timmy jumped up with his putter. "Let's go!" he yelled as he took off running with his club over his head directly towards some geese that were walking about 30 yards from the range. Nine other boys jumped up and joined in the pursuit, also brandishing miniature putters over their heads.

"Wait! Stop! Boys!" Chris took off after them, knowing geese can be very aggressive when threatened. Fortunately, geese are also able to walk fast and fly, which they did to avoid the screaming band of club-wielding 10 year olds.

46

Between the three of them, they could figure out most of the operational issues at the course. The one they couldn't figure out was maintaining the condition of the course.

Reversing years of neglect required more than just showmanship, and eventually, the novelty of the new attitude at Northcroft would wear off, and golfers would demand a good golfing experience to keep coming back. It was clear that they needed some outside help.

The first golf course consultant they brought in was named Dieter Haufman, whom Barry had found on the internet. His resume included work at some great Midwest courses, and his PowerPoint presentation on the Mac computer boasted some impressive promises.

"So that is our program," said at the conclusion of the show.

"Would you like to take a tour of the course now?" Paul asked.

Dieter put up his hand. "That is not necessary. Our program works under any circumstances."

"You don't need to even look at anything?"

"No."

After an awkward silence, Frank asked, "So what would it cost us to have you come in and get the course in shape?"

Dieter reached into his briefcase and pulled out a glossy page. He handed it to Frank, who in turn handed it to Paul, who then handed it to Barry. The price was almost a month's worth of greens fees.

"Thanks, Dieter. We'll be in touch."

The search would go on.

47

The man in the gray Chevy Tahoe that was parked down the block from Paul's house looked down to check his watch. It was almost midnight and he figured he'd give it another half hour or so before heading out.

Ten minutes later he noticed headlights coming up behind him and he crouched down to avoid being spotted, in the very unlikely event the driver would turn his head to look into a dark parked car. When the car slowed and turned into Paul's driveway, the man felt his pulse increase. Maybe this was finally the time.

He saw the driver get out of the car, walk around the back of the car, open the hatchback, and pull out a computer bag. The driveway was positioned perfectly for the streetlight to illumine the driver as he closed the back and walked up to the front door of the house.

It was not Paul Smith.

This man was short, maybe 5' 9"or so, with a dark complexion and black hair. He walked a little gingerly, like he had recently suffered a groin injury.

The man in the Tahoe waited a few minutes before driving away.

That's all right. He had time.

48

Jessica Weaver was trying to get Mrs. Laver to transfer her weight correctly.

"At the top of the backswing, most of your weight should be on your right foot, and specifically, the inside of your right foot. Then you shift your weight forward, so that at impact most of your weight is on your front foot, and on the follow-through your right foot comes almost all the way off the ground." She demonstrated slowly.

So what am I doing wrong?" Mrs. Laver asked.

"When you bring your club back, you shift your weight forward onto your front foot, which is logical - since you've moved your arms back, making you think you have to move your weight forward for balance. But that movement forces you to shift your weight backward, instead of forward, on the downswing, which saps your power. The golf swing requires just the opposite; you pull your arms back AND shift your weight back to load up for the forward action of the downswing."

"Golf is hard," Mrs. Laver said.

Jessica laughed. "You'll get it. You've made great progress already. Remember your first lesson?"

"Ugh. Don't remind me. I'm lucky to have such a great teacher," she said.

"I don't know about that. You're the one hitting the ball,' Jessica said. "Let's hit three more and end on a good one."

Jessica Weaver had not always wanted to be a golf pro. She had originally wanted to be a dancer, but that dream ended in junior high school when she realized there were too many other girls with a similar dream, girls that were just a little thinner, prettier, and, well, just better dancers than she was. It had surprised her at the time that revisioning her future at age thirteen hadn't been the devastating blow to her that it had been to some of the other girls, and she realized right then that being adaptable and accepting of change was the way to maintain happiness.

From the time she was little, her father had dragged her out with him to the driving range on Saturday mornings to give her mom some alone time, and while Jessica sat on the bench behind her dad pretending to be bored, she secretly found the people there fascinating. It reminded her of the zoo, where each animal looked and acted in a strange and unusual way. Even then, without any background, she appreciated an elegant swing, and the graceful arc of the golf ball that resulted from it. There was something pure about it - something true - that innately appealed to her. Conversely, the labored and struggling swings of the hackers - and the ugly shots they created – seemed to cry out for help.

When her father had 5 balls remaining, he'd call Jessica over, gently set her up in golf posture, and let her whale away at them. This was the highlight of her week – the two of them laughing at her misses, and cheering her good shots. At 11 she took some group lessons with her friends, then some individual lessons, but it was just something to do. The golf connection was more about being together with her dad. She tried out for and made the freshman golf team because it got her out of seventh and eight periods at school, but the team was kind of a joke and lost most of their matches.

It was during the summer prior to junior year that things changed. As her body developed she noticed how much power her solid legs provided, and the distance of her shots jumped dramatically. She started working diligently to refine her swing, not just to become a better golfer, but for the sheer aesthetic of it. Jessica noticed something else: as a tan, young sixteen year old girl on the driving range, she attracted a lot of attention.

Now, even at 34, that still seemed to be the case.

Barry waited until Mrs. Laver was out of earshot before walking over to Jessica. "She shifts her weight forward on the backswing."

"Hey, who's the pro here?" Jessica said.

"Sorry. You're the pro."

"You looking for another lesson?"

Barry looked over at other golfers to make sure they were out of earshot. "Uh, no. Actually, I was wondering if you were involved with anyone."

"You're supposed to ask what 'my situation' or 'my deal' is," she said. "That's how we do it in 2008."

"Ah. Okay. Good to know." She was not making this easy, he thought. "What is 'your situation?' "

"Are you asking as the owner, or for yourself?"

"Is the answer different?"

"No. And I'm not seeing anyone."

"Can I buy you dinner this Friday?"

"Sure."

Barry and Jessica sat at the new Mexican place had opened up near Northcroft, munching on the chips and salsa in front of them.

"As I'm sitting here I realize we have nothing in common, and technically I'm your boss," Barry said.

"So true. What could go wrong in this relationship?"

"Relationship? All I did was ask you to get some food with me. Plus I'm still extricating myself from my marriage, and that could get ugly."

"Wow, you're quite the salesman. Who wouldn't want to date you?"

"I'm just saying that I think you're terrific and all, but I don't know where this is going."

"I don't know where it's going either. But rather than see the finish line, why don't we take the trip together?"

"You're pretty smart for being just a kid."

"Look, everyone brings baggage to a relationship."

He laughed. "My baggage is a steamer trunk and footlocker, and yours is a…." Catching himself, he said, "You don't even know what those are!"

"I'm assuming they refer to some type of baggage?" she said.

"Yes. Like they carried on the Titanic."

"Oh, I loved that movie," Jessica said.

"Yeah, me, too. Anyway, in terms of baggage…"

Well, I was married once," Jessica said.

"Really?"

"Are you surprised anyone would marry me? Or that anyone would leave me?"

"I just didn't know that about you. It makes you more mysterious."

She just smiled at him. "I'm hungry. Let's order."

Barry smiled at Jessica and realized he was trying to talk himself, not her, out of the relationship, and it was not working. It had been a long time since he'd fallen for Rachel's smile, but there was just something about Jessica that drew him to her.

"Good idea. Let's eat," he said.

49

The next golf course consultant that Barry found on the internet, Noel Valentine, took a much different approach than Dieter Haufman.

"I like to get to know the course, you know, on a spiritual level," he told the men. "Each course has a unique wavelength, and to truly bring out its beauty I need to get on that wavelength."

"Would you like me to give you a tour?" Paul asked.

"Actually, if you don't mind, I'd like to walk around by myself for a while. I want to really listen to what it's telling me."

Paul shrugged. "Great. Let me know if you need anything."

The men watched at the clubhouse door as Noel headed down the 18th fairway back towards the far end of the course.

"Pony tail. Check. Birkenstock sandals. Check. Vest. Check." Frank said, "Am I missing anything?"

"Just a walking stick," Paul said.

"Hey, we need help," Barry said. "Let's give him a chance."

"You're right. Let's hope he's got the answer," Frank said.

About two hours later, Paul walked up to Frank on the 1st tee.

"Have you seen Noel?"

"No, actually I forgot about him," Frank said. "Where do you think he is?"

"I have no idea. Should we go look for him?" Paul asked.

"Nah, he'll turn up."

"If you say so."

At 4:30pm Noel walked into the clubhouse and found Frank and Barry. He had been gone for 3 and a half hours.

"Your course is very sad," Noel said. "I felt a lot of negative energy."

"Can you help us?" Barry asked. "Can you fix it?"

Noel smiled. "Of course. There are no bad courses, only courses that need a little more care."

"And what would that care entail, I mean cost-wise?"

Noel closed his eyes and thought for a moment, then opened them and smiled.

His price was less than Dieter's, but still more than the men could afford.

"Thanks. We'll be in touch."

They were running out of options.

50

Paul got off the Red Line stop on the El at Addison and rode the escalator down to street level. There were plenty of ticket sellers for the afternoon game against the Pirates and he bought a single grandstand seat for 75% of face value, not intending to use that location. He would find a seat with plenty of empties around to spread out and enjoy the day. He stood out only for his lack of any Cubs clothing or hats, and had no interest in a game program, the starting lineups, or the ceremonial first pitch.

For 40 years he and his friends had been coming to this so-called shrine of a ballpark, and he expected that familiarity to inspire the kind of introspection he needed today. Paul hated clichés, but the timelessness of Wrigley Field somehow encouraged clear thinking about the big things in life. The game was immortal, yet being played in the here and now. Although Paul didn't know it, Frank had come here after he'd passed on Carly's invitation, as had Barry after quitting his job via email.

Each year on opening week Cubs players left Arizona's

sunny Spring Training weather for the howling winds and gray afternoons of April in Chicago. What transpired at Wrigley during those frigid first few weeks often barely qualified as baseball. The month of May was only slightly better. June and July meant the reemergence of emerald green ivy on the wall, lazy afternoons of ballpark food, beer, and occasional feats of excellence on the field. During the 1990s, Cubs games during June took a back seat to Chicago Bulls playoff runs, a brief but sublime period in Chicago sports history. The reality of another pennantless season typically started to set in about August. Then September saw the team playing out the schedule, the players trying to get that extra hit to reach .300, or 30 homers, numbers that would look so much better on the back of next year's baseball card. For a tiny minority, that extra performance would be set down as part of their baseball legacy, maybe even leading to enshrinement in Cooperstown, or a retired uniform number. For everyone else, their statistical record would be a source of family pride, brought out like war medals or awards to celebrate on special occasions: "My uncle Bob played major league baseball!" The final month of a losing Cubs baseball season competed for attention with its mirror opposite, the hopeful beginnings of a Chicago Bears season. Despite the city's lack of championship banners, it was indeed a glorious cycle.

Paul leaned back with his feet up on the seat in front, letting the sun warm his mind as he thought about his situation. On the one hand, he no longer had the security of Candor Electric and a job he excelled at and enjoyed. He was divorced, with fortunately little contact with his ex-wife, and unfortunately little contact with his only daughter. His retirement funds were now invested in a venture with uncertain prospects. Oh, and a large, mysterious man was probably looking for him. He likened it to a bad Cubs team in April.

Then there was Julie. If the change in career was unsettling, his feelings for her were twice as disruptive. His life had been comfortable, without much concern for the future or for anyone else, actually. Now his relationship with her was becoming something real, something that called for an even greater investment than the one he'd put into Northcroft. Things with Julie felt right, but going any deeper would require the type of mental shift that most naturally people resist, which was why behavioral change is so difficult. Here he was, in his familiar surroundings, letting his mind catch up with his heart, which had already made the decision to move forward with Julie. Maybe it's a sign, he thought, that the only Cubs game he's actually attended this season involves a team from her home town of Pittsburgh.

He rose in the bottom of the sixth to remove himself from the suspended animation of the game and venture back into the reality of 2008.

If you're going to shake up your life, he thought, might as well do it all at once.

51

Larry Santi had been an average student, not particularly smart, and had spent a good part of his days at University of Illinois drinking beer. The summer after graduation he had worked for the Highmoor Park District cleaning up after picnickers. Then one of his father's friends got him a job as a runner down at the Chicago Board of Trade, back in the glory days when you could turn a small stake into a fortune. Working his way up into a trading role, Larry's short attention span and inability to foresee possible bad consequences turned out to be a perfect fit for the commodities pits, and he indeed turned a small stake into a fortune.

The best trade he ever made, though, was buying a few seat memberships on the Board when they temporarily got cheap, because in recent years, even as the trading business moved toward electronic transactions, the seats still commanded an exorbitant price from big institutional trading operations. Selling his seats had provided enough cash for Larry to spend his days at Hawthorne Country Club.

He'd married Debbie right before he'd hit it big, and he'd been mostly faithful to her over their 27 years together. Sure, there had been a few sexual encounters connected with bachelor parties or Las Vegas debauchery with his trading friends from the Board, but he figured that was just part of being a big-time commodity trader, an entitlement, so to speak. He kind of assumed Debbie knew about them, or at least suspected, and he had never felt any real guilt.

Rachel Conrad Stone, however, was a different story. He'd had a big crush on her since they were in college, and it had never gone away. He knew Rachel had been way too pretty to be interested in him back then – he'd been a little overweight, kind of a slob, really. Then Barry Stone had come along and married Rachel, and he'd taken a cushy job with Rachel's father, while Larry had headed down to the rough and tumble world of the trading pits. But now Barry was unemployed, or working at a golf course, or something like that. Anyway, it seemed like he was out of the picture, and Rachel was still a dark beauty, with that fabulous smile

I may be a little overweight, Larry thought, and mostly bald, but I'm rich, and maybe if I'm there for her during this difficult time, that might be enough to make Rachel Conrad see him as more than a friend, and scratch his thirty year itch.

Today he was driving his white Mercedes S550 – the white 'Vette was too conspicuous in case something happened later. He had told Debbie he was meeting an old college buddy, which in his mind was not really a lie. He pulled up to Rachel's house and walked up the steps to escort her to his car.

"Rachel opened the door and smiled. "Hi, Larry."

"You look fantastic," he said.

"Thank you."

They walked down to the car and Larry opened the door for her. "I made reservations at Gabriel's. It's the best French food there is."

"That's out of the way, isn't it?" Rachel said. "I've never been there."

"Nah, it's about 40 minutes. But it's worth it."

He climbed in the other side, hit the accelerator, and they sped off.

52

Frank was having a sandwich in the clubhouse when he got a call on the walkie talkie from Jimmy Boyle, who was filling in as starter on the first tee.

"Mr. Jordan?"

"What's up, Jimmy?"

"Um, do we, uh, have like a dress code, or something?"

"Why do you ask?"

"Well, um, there's a group here, and like, I'm not sure what to do."

"Are they dressed inappropriately?" He had Frank's attention.

"Um, they're like, from Hooters."

"I'll be right there." The sandwich could wait.

Sure enough, as Frank exited the clubhouse and headed for the first tee he saw a small crowd – of men, of course – watching as four girls in tight white T-shirts and tiny orange shorts took their "practice" swings. He made his way through the crowd and was greeted by a man with a camera hanging from his neck.

"Are you the club manager?"

"One of them," Frank said.

"I'm Pete Luglia. We thought with all the attention your course is getting we could help each other out, you know, promote each other's brands with a quick photo shoot." By this time two of the girls had walked over. "This is Tiffany, and this is Amber." The girls said hello to Frank.

"Sure, why not? Just keep it classy," Frank said. "How many holes are you going to play?"

"Oh, just one. We'll hit a few drives, a couple iron shots, maybe a sand shot or two, then some putting," Luglia said. "We'll be out of your way before you know it." Frank envisioned in his head what the photos would look like when the girls bent over to putt.

Right then one of the girls on the tee swung and cracked a drive right down the middle of the fairway, generating raucous applause from the crowd. Pete leaned over and whispered to Frank, "They're not all just eye candy. Some are pretty athletic."

Frank nodded. "So I see." Shaking his head, he went back into the clubhouse to finish his sandwich.

It was Frank's turn to close up, and it had been a good day at Northcroft. There had been lots of greens fees and they had almost sold out of women's shirts in the pro shop. He'd have to remind Barry to order those in the morning. Paul popped his head into the office.

"I'm heading out. Taking Julie to see 'Ironman' tonight."

"Hey, Paul I'm glad you stopped in. I saw you fixed the fuse box for the parking lot floodlight. That will keep our relations good with the insurance company."

Paul looked quizzical. "I didn't fix that. Are you sure it's working now?"

"Yeah, I noticed it last night."

"Huh."

"Maybe Jimmy did it."

"Maybe," Paul said.

"Well, it's working again." Frank returned to his deskwork. "Enjoy Ironman."

"Yeah, thanks," Paul said. An interesting theory about the magically repairing fuse box came to him as he walked to his car.

53

Julie and Paul walked out of the Cineplex and headed to his van.

"What did you think?" he asked.

"I liked it, but shouldn't Gwyneth Paltrow be getting bigger parts?" she replied. "That was a small supporting role. Isn't she still a big star?"

"Good point. It wasn't a big role, but it was a blockbuster movie, probably be the biggest of 2008. Maybe some women are willing to take a lesser role to be part of something big. I guess you're not one of those," he kidded.

"Are you telling me you're actually a super hero in disguise? Mild-mannered electrician by day, crime fighter by night?"

"The only crime fighting I've done recently is when I clocked your ex-husband and his big friend. Speaking of which I guess his friend has given up his quest for revenge. Like I told you he would."

"I hope you're right about that," she said.

"So you think I'm mild-mannered?"

Julie cocked her head and looked at him. "Yes, I do. But in a good way. You don't get too high or too low."

They climbed into the van and rode in silence for a while, listening to the oldies station on Paul's radio. Julie preferred up-to-date music, like Rihanna and Lady Gaga, but the rule they had was that the driver got to pick the station. If there was one thing about Paul that gave her concern, it was his affinity for things from the past – songs, movies, even friends. She thought you could respect the past, as long as you didn't live in it. So far Paul had seemed to maintain a balance; he never talked about Viet Nam (except that once) or his failed marriage.

Paul turned down the radio and said to her, "I was watching Casablanca on TV a couple nights ago. My favorite movie. Humphrey Bogart, Claude Raines, Ingrid Bergman. Fantastic script. Anyway, I'm watching all these extras in the background – the German officers, the band that plays La Marseilles, the people in Rick's – and it occurs to me that 70 years ago or so they were all just actors showing up for work on the set, trying to make a living. They got up, went to work, put on their costumes, and when they were done filming they all just went home at the end of the day. Just like we do."

"So?"

"So, I'm thinking, here's all these actors, just doing their jobs, and not one of them is alive today."

"That's a morbid thought," Julie said.

"Just hear me out. The movie, Casablanca, is immortal, it lives on forever. But the people that made it, well, they're just like you and me. They're not immortal. All the worries they had about paying the bills, fighting with their families, all of it, just doesn't matter one bit today. We live our lives, do our best to be good people, but ultimately nothing we do is forever. We're just passing through. And if you remember that, nothing that happens day to day will get you all upset."

Sometimes Julie wasn't sure if Paul was full of deep thoughts, or full of something else.

There were still 3 pieces of pizza left on the tray when Julie said, "That's enough for me."

"What, no dessert?" Paul said.

"Are you kidding?"

"Come on, you can have a little dessert," he said, signaling the waiter over. "One piece of cheesecake, please, with the special topping."

"You're going to eat a piece of cheesecake now? You're crazy."

"The cheesecake's for you. I think you'll like the special topping."

"I'm not having any cheesecake. You ordered it, you eat it," Julie said.

"Maybe you'll change your mind."

"I doubt it. I don't want…." Julie stopped mid-sentence as the waiter placed a piece of cheesecake in front her, with the special topping Paul ordered.

It was an engagement ring.

She looked down, looked up at Paul, and leapt across the table to hug him.

"Yes!"

54

Dean Conrad was in a foul mood as he headed out for lunch.

The recession was taking its toll on Conrad & Co., and Barry Stone's abrupt departure had caused several accounts to move their accounting business to other firms. Though he hated to admit it, Barry had been more valuable to the firm than Dean had given him credit for.

Dean drove over to Ben's Deli and ordered a pastrami sandwich, chips, and a pickle. He sat down and opened the newspaper to take his mind off work for a while.

About 10 minutes later a white Corvette pulled into the parking lot. Larry Santi walked in, ordered tuna salad on wheat, with fries, and sat down at Dean's table.

"What did you find out from your friend at the bank?" Dean asked.

Larry smiled. "You're going to like this."

55

Kate Jordan had never been a big spender on clothes, but now she was being especially careful with her purchases.

Frank was always a good provider, and they had had very few serious fights about money. Most of their financial discussions had been in jest – he'd threaten to buy a new set of golf clubs if she bought the top-of-the-line espresso maker, or she'd threaten to redo the landscaping if he bought Bears' season tickets. But now, despite Frank's assurances that everything was okay monetarily, she could sense more than a little worry in her husband.

In fact, Kate had always been able to read Frank, going all the way back to their dating days at Wash U in the 70's. That was when people first started to realize that not all jocks were dumb, and it was immediately apparent that there was more to Frank Jordan than just a football helmet. While Kate had been cute in college, she was not one of the really pretty popular girls back then. But as she had matured into her 30s and 40s, she had maintained her natural good looks, while many of her contemporaries either quit trying, or "had work done."

Right out of college she became an elementary school teacher, worked for four years before becoming a full time mother, and then returned to work as a teacher's aide at Jefferson Elementary. It paid little, but the kids and teachers all loved "Mrs. J."

As she left Macy's on the upper level of LakeTown Mall, she heard someone calling her name. "Kate?"

She turned to see Michelle Schafer coming out of Neiman Marcus. Michelle's son Troy had been a baseball teammate of Nate Jordan.

"Hi, Michelle. How are you?"

"Busy! So busy! Things never seem to slow down."

Kate noticed Michelle was so busy that she had an armful of Neiman Marcus shopping bags, but kept that to herself. She asked, "Are you still on the hospital board?"

"Ugh. Yes. We had our big gala last month. Raised almost a quarter of a million dollars, even in this economy. Can you believe it? But it was SO much work. Now I'm hosting this big dinner for Tom and all the partners at his law firm."

"Wow, that must be a big job. Don't they have assistants to do all that?" Kate asked, well knowing the answer.

"Oh they do, they do, but Tom wanted more of an upscale touch." She raised her package-laden arms. "So here I am."

"Well, I'm sure it will be a big success with you at the helm."

"I heard about Frank. I'm so sorry. Has he found anything yet?"

"Actually he and a couple of partners bought a golf course."

"Really? A golf course?" Michelle's disappointment that Frank owned a golf course was obvious.

"Yes. In Lake View."

"Doesn't that require a lot of money?" The implication being that the Jordans couldn't afford a golf course.

"I suppose, although they got a great deal. Anyway, they did it. Frank's really enjoying it, too. You should have Tom come by to play," Kate said. She knew Tom Schaefer would never play a public course.

"Ugh. Tom has no time to play. He's got this big project for a developer. It's going to reshape the whole city. It's huge."

"That sounds great, Michelle," Kate said. "How are your kids?"

"Everyone's great. Troy got into business school at Northwestern so he's all excited about that. Sheila just loves being a mom – and I absolutely love being a grandmother – and oh, he is just the cutest baby in the world. We have, like 500 photos of him. And Alice will be a senior at Wellesley; hopefully graduating with honors next year."

"Well, good for them. So nice to see you and catch up, Michelle."

"You, too, Kate. Bye."

Kate couldn't get away quickly enough.

56

Barry walked into the Northcroft office where Frank and Paul were waiting.

"Okay, here's where we stand," he said, looking at the spreadsheet he was holding. "We're just about breakeven. The interest on the bank note is a big nut every month, and there's not much we can do about that. We're all taking very modest salaries…"

"I can make more by just doing three wiring jobs," Paul interrupted.

Barry ignored him. "…and I can't see cutting back much on maintenance, not with the course looking the way it does."

"So what's the takeaway?" Frank asked.

Barry put the paper down. "The takeaway is that we're barely making it. The numbers aren't great but over time, if bookings increase, I think we'll be all right."

It was silent for a few moments, then Barry shrugged and said, "I can live with 'all right.'"

"Me, too," Frank said.

"I guess it beats working for somebody else," Paul said.

There's not many people in the world that can tee off on a golf course they actually own. On a mild summer night the three owners set off to enjoy a quick round.

Frank's drive on the par 4 seventh hole found the left rough, and Paul followed him there. Barry's drive split the fairway 25 yards past them.

"It's all brown here, Paul. Do you have any ideas on this? The 12th fairway looks even worse."

"I know. I've tried a few things but nothing's worked."

"The doctors really let this thing go. I hope we can figure out a way to fix it," Frank said.

"I do have one idea, but I wanted to run it by you guys first," Paul said.

Barry yelled over. "Are you guys going to play, or what?"

Frank stepped up to his ball, went through his routine, and hit his ball to the back of the green. "Whatever your idea is, I'm open to it."

As the three approached the ninth green, Frank whispered to Paul, and both men started chuckling.

"What?" Barry asked.

"Nothing."

"No, what is it? I want to know."

Frank and Paul looked at each other.

"Of course you're playing great. You spend all the time on the range with Jessica," Frank said.

"What are you talking about? I don't spend that much time with Jessica."

"Does she charge you by the hour, or do you take it out in trade?"

"You're sick. She's 34 years old and a total

professional. We're just friends."

"Yes, I'm sure she's professional. And I'm sure she's 34."

Paul joined in. "We have another professional, you know. Chris Keller gives lessons, too."

"Yes, thanks for the tip," Barry said, immediately regretting it.

"Speaking of tips, are you giving some to Jessica?"

"Does she have nice tips?"

Barry ignored them as he lined up his next shot, which ended up in the middle of the green about 8 feet from the hole. Paul was short left and Frank was in the right sand trap.

"Well whatever she's doing, it's sure working," Frank said.

A few holes later, after more jokes had been made, Barry said, "I know you make jokes and all, but let me let you guys something. Everything she says about golf swing is really about me. Sometimes I hold on too tight. Sometimes I don't have trust in my swing, so I don't release the club. When something's wrong I over-correct. I always think long term, so I'm not in the moment on each shot. It's like all the things in my life that are wrong are reflected in my golf swing. And one by one, she's helping me eliminate them from my game. And my life."

Frank and Paul remained silent. Barry was absolutely right about all of it, and they had to admit it they'd seen positive change in their lifelong friend. Both on the golf course, and off it.

Barry continued. "Rachel and I looked great on paper, and don't get me wrong, I loved her. I still do. She's the mother of my children. But I was not my best when we were together. Sure, Dean was a big part of it. But not all of it. Some of it was just me. Uncle Vic talked about how I

201

used to see the whole field. Well, I am doing that again now, and it's helping me be, I don't know, just better."

The three putted out in silence, and walked to the next tee.

"Plus you get to nail a 34-year-old," Paul said.

"Shut up."

57

The man slipped through the fence near the 14th hole and made his way purposely towards his destination. In his pocket was a device he'd crafted in his workshop, and tonight he'd put it into service.

The blackness was almost total but he deftly avoided a rake which was left outside the sand trap on the eleventh hole as he crossed the fairways. He gently placed the rake back inside the trap.

"Can I give you a lift?"

Tommy G spun around to see a man sitting in a golf cart about 20 yards behind him, between Tommy and the fence. His first instinct was to run, but he was too old for that. Plus, run where? The man was positioned to block his retreat. Tommy had missed him coming through the fence because of a big ash tree. Now his mind started to work. Was it police? Private security? He was trespassing, big deal, what were they going to do? Finally curiosity replaced alarm. Who was in the cart?

Paul pulled the cart up to Tommy. "Hop in."

Tommy stood still for just a moment, sizing up the situation. Then he climbed into the golf cart with his tools on his lap.

"Nice night," Paul said.

Tommy mumbled, "I guess."

"Where to, Mr. G?"

After a long pause, Tommy said, "Sprinkler head in the middle of the seventh fairway."

Tommy went to work replacing the sprinkler head with the one he'd adapted in his home shop, while Paul knelt nearby.

"This fairway lies at the low point here, and the sleeve that holds the head has been bent over time by the carts, so the head can't retract properly and the water can't flow right," Tommy explained. "I made this one with a spring that will retract and maintain water pressure, even when it gets run over." He stood up. "You see, it looks like the lowest point is over there by the 12th green, but it's not. It's right here."

"You'd never be able to tell that," Paul said.

"Exactly. You have to know the course," Tommy said proudly.

They climbed back into the cart and Paul headed to the clubhouse. It was obvious that they weren't headed back to the fence where Tommy had made his entry, but he didn't seem to mind. If fact, he started to open up.

"Over there on seventeen we had to build up the tee box because you couldn't tell when the fairway was clear. We thought about putting in a big bell like they have at some courses but I thought that was stupid. Then over there on four we put in the oval sand trap because too many yahoos were trying to cut it and go for the green off the tee." He chuckled. "One November I found 165 balls in the woods back there. Gave 'em all to the kids."

At the clubhouse Paul went in and grabbed a six pack, and when he came out they sat on the patio. Tommy needed little coaxing to wax eloquent on the layout and eccentricities of Northcroft, so Paul waited for his opening. Finally, Tommy took a long pull on his beer and seemed to be satisfied.

"We're really trying hard to bring the course back to life," Paul said. "Some of the things are working, some not so well."

Tommy nodded but said nothing.

"Anyway, the electrical company I worked for went under, my friend quit his accounting job, and my other friend lost his job in the markets."

"Yeah, the markets are tough right now."

Paul was a little surprised Tommy would follow the markets but figured it had been a big enough news story in the popular press.

"So we bought this course from the doctors…"

Tommy grunted. "The doctors. They almost destroyed this place. They had no feeling for it at all. Why would you buy a beautiful golf course and not take care of it. I'll never understand that." He shook his head.

"Yeah, they are an interesting bunch. Anyway, like I said, most of the stuff is going well. But I'm a little overmatched by the actual maintenance of the grounds themselves."

"Of course. Gotta know the land."

Paul wasn't really sure what Tommy was thinking. I mean, here was a guy who was sneaking on the course at night to repair things, so clearly he was emotionally invested in the course. Yet he didn't seem to be biting at the lines Paul was tossing him. It didn't matter – Paul needed Tommy, so he was going to have to draw him out.

"You know the land," Paul said.

"That's true."

They were silent for a few minutes, then Tommy said, "There was this great old guy, Andy Olin, that used to play here with his brother Robert when I was just starting out. I was never really sure what he did for a living – he was some kind of wheeler-dealer, you know the type. And he always had money. Anyway, he took a liking to me and we used to talk after his rounds. One day, he puts his arm around me and he gets really serious. 'Tommy,' he says, 'I want you to do something for me.' 'Sure, Mr. Olin' I says. He says, 'Robert and I are going to buy some buildings in Chicago, around Wrigley Field, and I want you to go in with us.' Now I didn't have much back then, but he made me promise. So every paycheck I'd send him some money to put into the buildings. Now this was the 1970s, remember, and the area around Wrigley was pretty run down. Plus, there was a lot of gang activity there, with the Latin Kings, and all them. Heck, I didn't even know what I was doing, but I trusted Mr. Olin, so I did it."

"So you own real estate in Wrigleyville?" Paul asked.

"Well, not anymore. When the Olin boys moved to Arizona they wanted to cash out, so we did. Didn't get the very top of the market, but we did pretty good."

Paul sat back to digest what he'd just heard.

Tommy stood up. "Thanks for the beer."

Paul stood up and they shook hands. "Can I give you a lift back to the fence?"

"Nah." Tommy smiled. "I know the way."

He was about 30 feet away when Paul called him.

"Hey, Tommy?"

He turned around.

"I need to talk to my partners, but what would you say…"

Tommy laughed. "I'll be here at 6 tomorrow. I was getting tired of sneaking around anyway. Thanks again for the beer." And off he went to the fence.

58

September, 2008

Tommy's return seemed to energize everyone at Northcroft. His former assistant Jimmy Boyle had been especially relieved that Tommy was back, and took to his duties with new enthusiasm. Tommy had requested just a token salary, plus picking up his healthcare insurance. Given what he'd told Paul about his real estate investing, just how much money did our groundskeeper have was a popular, but unspoken question.

With his crowded lesson schedule and the success of the junior golf program, Chris Keller was happily on the range from morning until dusk. Jessica also had a spring in her step, which could be attributed not only to her full lesson slate, but also to her new relationship.

Bookings were increasing, and with the course looking greener , the course didn't require the previous discounts and gimmicks. Frank especially appreciated not having to risk any more curfew violations. Barry even showed a surprising knack for merchandising the pro shop, and with Jessica's help that area was becoming more profitable.

At 3:30pm one Friday there was an opening, so Frank, Paul, and Barry slipped out to play the back nine.

As they walked off the 18th green, their attorney, Arthur Brinkman was waiting for them.

Barry was the first to realize this wasn't a happy occasion.

"Hi, Arthur. What's up?"

"Let's go into the office."

After they assembled, he broke the story.

"The bank sold the note on the course."

When no one spoke, Arthur continued. "The way these things are structured, the noteholder can accelerate payment if any of the covenants are violated."

Frank and Paul looked at Barry, who said, "Theoretically we're in violation of the cash flow to debt ratio. Just by a little. The bank never cares about those ratios as long as we make the payments on time. The covenants are just in there in case they sense things are going sour quickly."

Arthur said, "That's exactly right. The bank doesn't care. Of course, the new noteholder might."

"I don't have any more money to put into this to buy the note," Paul said.

"I'm tapped, too," Barry added.

Frank thought a moment. "Yeah, we can't pay off the note right now, even though things are going good. No way we can come up with that."

"I'm not done," Arthur said.

"Oh, now for the bad news, Arthur?" Paul quipped.

"Yes. The buyer of the note is Dean Conrad."

59

The last time they'd met at Paul's house like this it was to decide to go forward with the Northcroft purchase. This time, it was to lament the impending loss of control of their business.

"It's my fault. This is about me and Rachel and Dean," Barry said.

"I blame the bank," Paul said. "I mean we were making the payments. Why do they care about the whatever-it-was ratio? I don't understand."

"The banks are all scared now. Especially the little hometown ones. They can't have any suspect loans on the books right now. The Feds are all over them to make sure every loan is clean," Frank said.

"That's ridiculous. I've never welched on a loan in my life," Paul said.

"That's not the point."

"What is the point?" Paul yelled. "What is the point? We turned that lousy place around and now we just give it to Dean Conrad?"

"We're not giving it to him - he'll just hold a majority stake."

"Oh, so we'll work for him? No thanks," Paul said.

"We might have to work for him for a little while, just until we can negotiate a decent sale price for our shares," Frank said. "If we bail completely the place will blow up and we'll get nothing. Or very little."

"Screw him," Paul said. "If I lose, I lose."

Barry said, "Money is a little dicey for me right now. I can't afford to just let this go."

"You want to work for Dean again?" Paul asked. "Come on."

"No, I don't want to work for Dean again. I'm just saying it's a little different for me. You know, with the separation and everything."

Paul turned to Frank. "You gonna work for Dean Conrad, Frank?"

"No. But I want to get maximum value for my shares. I need that money, too.

"I don't believe this."

"We're just being careful here, Paul. Trying to make the best of a bad situation," Barry said.

Paul stood up. "I'm going to piss."

After he left, Frank said, "How bad is your financial situation?

Barry took a deep breath. "Bad. The timing on this couldn't be worse."

"This is gonna hurt me, too. We have to cut the best deal we can. We do have some leverage - after all, Dean can't run the course on his own."

Barry nodded. "That's probably the best plan. I just wish we had another idea."

"Me, too.

Paul returned, and they turned on the TV for a little diversion, but nothing could lift their spirits. The three couldn't even muster their usual banter. Although they were seated together in Paul's den, each man was mentally in his own world, going through worst-case scenarios and not finding much hope.

Around midnight, Barry got up to leave.

"I'm going over to Jessica's."

"I'll walk out with you." Frank stood up and followed him.

At the door the three hugged briefly, and with nothing more to say, Frank and Barry headed to their cars. Paul stood at the door and watched them drive off, as did the large man in the gray Tahoe parked a few doors down. The man waited 5 minutes, then removed the 9mm pistol from the case on the passenger seat, stuck it behind him in his belt, and made his way up the sidewalk to Paul's front door.

Paul had turned off the TV and was picking up the leftover pizza boxes when the doorbell rang. He assumed one of them had left their cellphone. Julie was staying at her place tonight to give the men some space. Maybe she was coming by to surprise or him and to cheer him up. He doubted that would work.

He was startled to open the door to a large black man.

"Paul Smith." It wasn't a question.

Paul didn't respond.

"I've been looking for you."

60

Paul and the large visitor stood at the door staring at each other, and then the man reached into his jacket. When he pulled his hand out it contained an old black and white photograph, which he handed to Paul.

He looked at the photo for a minute, then at the face of the visitor.

"I'm Don Edwards," the man said.

Paul felt like the wind had been knocked out of him. He looked down at the picture. In the group shot he saw himself at nineteen, a kid with no sense of what life would hold for him. And standing in the upper left corner he saw a thin black kid from Detroit, Michigan who loved cars.

He looked up from the photo at the man's face. "You got fat."

Don Edwards' face broke into a large grin. "So you don't think you could carry me across that field anymore?"

Paul smiled. "I didn't want to carry you the first time. I stepped on you by accident."

Don stepped forward and the two embraced.

"I can't believe it. Don Edwards."

"It's me."

"Come in. Sit down," Paul said. "Can I get you a beer?"

"That would be great."

The two men sat down and looked at each other for the first time in 38 years.

"Don Edwards. From Detroit, Michigan."

"Yes. Detroit, Michigan. I'm still there. Of course, things are a little different for me now." Don told Paul about getting out of the Army and returning home, getting his first real job selling Buicks, and how he now owned four Chevrolet dealerships in Michigan.

"I used to own six dealerships, but this recession, man, it's just devastated the car business. We had to sell a couple. Broke my heart."

"I remember that you always loved cars. We used to talk about that on patrol breaks."

"Yeah, well it worked out. Detroit still has plenty of problems, but for me, it's always been home." He pulled out his gun and put it on the sofa beside him. "Of course, I carry this around just in case. Where I'm from you have to look out for yourself."

"You've been armed ever since I've known you. Why change now?"

Don laughed, and Paul figured it was the kind of laugh that naturally happy people have.

"It's not the M16s we used to carry, but it's gotten me out of a few jams," Don said.

"I'll bet. Are you married? Have kids?"

"Thirty-four years this December. I met Ruth when she came in to buy a Chevy Impala. Sold her a beautiful navy blue model. We filled out all the paperwork, and I handed her the keys. I told her 'This model comes with a little extra personal service.'" He laughed again. "At first she thought I was just fooling around, but eventually she let me take her out proper." He reached in to pull out his wallet for a picture and started pointing. "There's Anthony, and Thomas, they work with me at the dealerships, and that's Ruthie, and this is Lisa, she's at Michigan State, and this is Susan, she's a nurse, and this is Paul, he's a Wayne County Sheriff."

"Paul, huh? Good name. And he's a cop."

"A Sheriff."

"Five kids? You're a lucky man."

"I am. I feel blessed every day. So tell me about you."

Paul related the story of his long career as an electrician, his failed marriage, his estranged daughter, his recent adventure with Northcroft, and his relationship with Julie.

Handing Don another beer, Paul asked, "So why are you showing up now?"

Don took a long pull on his beer. "Five months ago I had a health scare. I don't like talking about the details, but something like that changes the way you look at things. I'm a workaholic, always have been, but after I got out of the hospital Ruthie made me scale back hours, and for the first time ever I had some free time. One day I'm down in the basement going through some old boxes I didn't even know I still had, and I came across some old pictures from my time in the service. Like this one." He pointed to the photo Paul was still holding. "And there you were. So I got to thinking, I gotta find that man. So my daughter helped me with a Google search and I started to track you down. You know how many Paul Smiths there are in the Chicago area? One hundred and thirty-five. So it took me a while. I made 3 trips over here, even after I narrowed it down."

"Why didn't you just use a private investigator? Save you time and," Paul smiled, "...obviously you can afford it."

"Yeah, that's what my boys said. But this was something I wanted to do myself. I never had much growing up, you know, and I earned everything I have the hard way. Plus all the time I was on the road, and tracking down the other Paul Smiths, it gave me time to think about things, you know? I mean, when you're building a business, and raising a family there's just no time to stop and think about how you got here, all the people in your life that made a difference. The good, and the bad. Anyway, I just wanted to find you on my own." Don's eyes misted up, and he leaned forward. "And I did."

Paul's eyes also misted up. "I'll drink to that."

They talked about Blackhawks and Red Wings, Bears and Lions, Cubs and Tigers. After another hour or so, the talk took a serious turn.

"You think much about your time over there?" Don asked.

"Not really," Paul said. "I've always been able to kind of, I don't know, shut out the bad things in life that have happened to me. That really helped out with my divorce. That was tough. Plus I was so young back when I was in country. I really didn't know what to think about anything, other than trying to stay alive."

"I was the same way – 'always push forward, don't look back,' at least until my health problem. And then when I found that old photo…"

"So now you're on a nostalgia tour?"

"I don't know about that. But I did want to find you. That's different. I owed you."

To keep himself together emotionally, Paul needed to change the subject. "Did you ever keep in touch with any of the guys in the unit?"

Don smiled. "Do you remember Oscar?"

"Oh yeah. He was from Detroit, too. Right?"

"He was. Remember how he used to sing those Motown songs all the time?"

"In that high voice!" Paul added. "We said he was one of the Supremes."

Don laughed. "Yes! He and I hung out a while after we got back. Then I lost track of him for about 10 years. One day about seven, eight years ago he came in to one of the dealerships. We got together for lunch once." Don looked at the label on his beer bottle. "Things hadn't worked out so well for him."

Paul said, "Do you remember that guy from New York, with the thick accent? What was his name?"

"Crovetti, Crovellini?"

"Crovelli! Dante Crovelli!" Paul said.

"Dante Crovelli. Couldn't understand a word he said," Don said.

"He had like, a hundred relatives. And who was the guy from California? You know the really tall, thin guy?"

"Oh, I know who you mean. He was really homesick. He missed the beach."

"Boy, I haven't thought about those guys in years," Paul said. And while he was glad to see the man whose life he saved so long ago, he didn't really want to think about the other guys tonight. Especially the ones who didn't make it back.

"So tell me more about this golf course you run with your friends."

"Well, that could be a short story." Paul told him about Dean Conrad's purchase of the note, how they probably would lose the course, and that Don had shown up right after they had resigned themselves to that fate.

"How much do you have come up with?" Don asked.

Paul told him and Don whistled. "That's a big number."

"Yeah." Paul took a swig of beer.

61

Dean Conrad hung up the phone.

"The meeting is tomorrow at 2 at Arthur Brinkman's office. Do you want to come?"

Rachel thought for a moment. "Should I? I don't know. I mean I'll come if you want me to. But I don't want to say the wrong thing."

"There is no wrong thing. They won't have the money to pay off the note, and we'll take over the course. Simple as that," Dean assured his daughter.

"I know. I just don't want to come off as a heartless bitch. I mean, Barry is the father of my children."

"I'm the one who comes off as the bad guy, honey. Not you."

"I guess."

"I'm only doing this for you, you know that."

"Seems like you're also doing it to get back at Barry for walking out of the company. Isn't there a little bit of truth in that, Dad?"

Dean leaned forward in his chair and pointed his finger at her. "Listen, I treated that son-of-a-bitch great all these years and how does he repay me? By quitting via an email that goes out to the whole company! And everybody I know found out. Just last week at the country club Marc Levin comes up to me in the locker room and says to me, 'I have to drop out of our golf date next week. Oh, I guess I should've emailed you.' Everybody got a big laugh out of that. Well, no one does that to Dean Conrad."

Rachel actually thought that Levin's comment was kinda funny, but knew better than to smile. Her father's status at Bellwood Country Club was a very sensitive topic to him, and somehow the manner in which his soon-to-be ex-son-in-law had departed his firm had quickly spread among the members. One's standing at Bellwood was dependent on a complex formula which included how much money you had, how well your children were doing, your golf or tennis proficiency, what your spouse (first or second) looked like, and if you held an executive position at the club. No one knew exactly how the formula worked but it seemed to regularly produce a clear pecking order, albeit a fluid one. On top of Barry's recent affront, Rachel knew that her father had recently lost an executive board seat election to Vic Lewis.

Dean said, "Anyway, we'll see who's laughing tomorrow."

"You never really warmed up to Barry," Rachel said. "Not that it matters now."

Dean came around the desk and put his arm around his daughter. "It's not that I didn't like him, honey. He's just not good enough for you. He never was. You deserve the very best."

She put her head on her father's shoulder. "You just say that because you're my dad."

"No, I say it because it's true. I'm your father and it's my job to take care of you. Trust me, honey. This is for the best."

"What are we going to do with the golf course?"

"Ah, I'm glad you asked!" Dean went back behind his desk and grabbed a file folder. "You and I are going to form a partnership and we're going to sell the course to some developers I know. And we're going to make a pile of money doing it."

"Okay, Dad. I'll be at the meeting tomorrow."

"Good. Tomorrow's going to be a great day for us."

62

Frank stood on his patio with a coffee mug in his hand. He'd checked the stock futures markets on CNBC (an old habit) and seen another big decline in the indexes. This was shaping up to be the worst year for the markets – and the economy – in decades. It hadn't been a great year in the Jordan house either, and what little positive they'd had – Northcroft's success – now looked to be crumbling with everything else.

The Blackberry in his pocket buzzed, and he answered it.

"Hello?"

"Hey Frank, it's Walter."

"Hi Walter, what's up?"

"I think I might have something for you. Can we meet this morning?"

"Sure. Where's good for you?"

"How about Starbuck's on Randolph at 10?"

"See you there, Walter."

Frank hung up and put the phone back in his pocket. Suddenly, things were looking up.

He sat at a table near the window looking out at the people at work.

The police officer, he didn't care about the financial recession, Frank thought. He'll make the same money no matter what. Maybe with things in the economy so bad crime would increase, and he'd have more work to do, but there wouldn't be any big bonus, maybe just a little overtime pay. How about the UPS delivery man? Frank thought they made pretty good money. The recession would probably reduce the number of packages he had to deliver, but his pay would be the same. In the old days he could most likely work his route just a little slower, deliver fewer packages in the same time, but today every single envelope and box would be coded and tracked, so he probably had to hustle to get them to their destinations.

But the salesmen he saw walking to their appointments, now they would certainly feel the recession. Frank searched their faces for any kind of indication that things were rough, but these urban workers maintained the same expression in good times or bad. It would be much later, say at 6 or 7pm, when they got back home to their house or apartment, that the strain would start to show. The strain of wondering how they'd meet their sales quota this month, how long they could hold onto their jobs with business so bad. Hell, some of these people I'm looking at might even be on their way to a meeting like the one I had with Magro, where I was told my services were no longer wanted, Frank thought.

Walter's arrival chased these dismal thoughts from Frank's head. He waved and Walter waved back as he stepped up to the counter to order. A few minutes later he took his cup from the barista, added some cream and sugar, and walked over to Frank's table.

"So, how's the golf course business?"

"Things are going well. It's a nice change from the financial markets."

"You call in sick today?"

"Something like that," Frank said.

"My friends that play there say the course looks great and it's usually crowded." Walter took a sip of coffee. "You guys have engineered a nice turnaround."

"Why don't you come see for yourself? Oh, that's right. You only play country club courses," Frank ribbed.

"Hey, I'll play anywhere. I'm friends with the owner of Northcroft but has he ever invited me to play? No! Not even once."

"Walter, you have a standing invitation. You can have any tee time you want, as long as it's before 6am and after 7pm."

"My favorite times!" Walter laughed.

"So you said you have something interesting for me," Frank said.

"Yes, but before we get into that, I need to know what happened at All American. I can't put you up for another job if you're going to pull out again."

Frank looked out the window and debated how to answer him. "There was a little more to the story there, Walter. The job definitely looked good on paper, but I wasn't sure about the office dynamics."

"You mean Carly."

"Basically, yeah."

Walter sat back, folded his hands, and looked at Frank. "Is there more to tell?"

Frank thought hard for a moment. "No. Nothing more. But I can assure you if you put me up for another job I won't embarrass you. You have my word."

Walter looked him in the eye for a moment, and then nodded. "Okay. What do you know about a hedge fund called Pegasus?"

"Are those the guys who left Morgan Stanley?"

"Yes, some of them, anyway. They started out by getting short the market right out of the chute and so they're just killing it this year. They're swamped and need help. I thought it might be a good fit for you."

"Sounds great, Walter. What do I need to do?"

"Well, first I needed to find out what happened at All American. Check. Now, I need to know if you're committed to the golf thing."

"I'm not sure the golf thing is the long term solution. I mean it's been great in the interim, but a good hedge fund job, those are hard to pass up. Can you just give me a day or two to talk to my partners?"

"I can hold off making the call for a couple days. Let me know as soon as you can." They talked about the markets for a while more, and finished their coffee.

At the door, Frank said, "I really appreciate you thinking of me. It means a lot."

"We go way back, Frank. Happy to help."

They shook hands and just as Walter started turned to walk away he stopped and turned back.

"By the way, one of the senior partners at All American ran into Carly Black in Vegas. She was meeting up with their top bond salesman for more than just an account review. That doesn't fly at that firm. It would be too messy to get rid of her now, but they'll move her out as soon as they can. Can you believe that?"

Frank assumed it was a rhetorical question and kept quiet.

"Well, I look forward to hearing from you soon," Walter said. "Pegasus is a fantastic opportunity."

63

Arthur Brinkman escorted Dean, Rachel, and their attorney Brian West into the conference room. Frank was standing at the window and Barry was seated. He rose to give Dean a cursory greeting, then turned to his soon-to-be ex-wife. "Hello, Rachel."

"Hi, Barry," she acknowledged with a small smile.

The Conrad team took their places across the table as Frank sat down. "Are we missing someone?" West asked Arthur.

"Yes, I'm sorry. Mr. Smith will be here shortly."

"Did he go to Washington?" Dean cracked, to the amusement of only himself and West, although Arthur gave a polite smile.

After a few silent minutes Paul strode in the room, followed by Don Edwards. Dean leaned over and whispered to West, who shrugged and shook his head. Don's presence was a surprise, and attorneys don't like surprises. Rachel snuck a peek at Barry and saw he was looking at her, as well.

Arthur opened, "I believe you have an action regarding

the note on Northcroft Golf Course?"

"Yes, we do," West began as he sent copies sliding down the long conference table.

"Persuant to section 5.1 titled "cash flow test", the audited accounting statements reveal a ratio below the rate required to be in good standing. Thus, pursuant to section 9.7 the noteholder, DJ Conrad & Co., is demanding full payment of the note, or surrender of the deed held by Northcroft Golf Partners, LLC."

Everyone at the table took a few moments to review the documents, except for Rachel, who continued to look at Barry.

"What is the current balance due on the note?" Arthur asked.

West reached into his briefcase and pulled out a piece of paper, showed it to Dean, who nodded, and then passed the paper to Arthur.

"So we're in agreement. Either you pay me the note balance or give me the deed." Dean had regained his bearing. Smiling, he added, "And you three don't have the dough."

Don let the words hang in the air for effect, then gently said, "But I do."

Dean looked at Don. "Who the hell are you?"

Don looked directly at Dean as Arthur filled in the blanks. "Mr. Edwards is an investor from Detroit who has arranged financing to pay off the note in full. Per section 10.8 he has until Friday to deposit the funds, which he has assured me will happen."

"What?!" Dean yelled. He turned to West. "What the hell is going on?!"

Arthur passed some papers over to West and Dean, which they hurriedly pored over. West turned white as he realized his client had been ambushed while Dean's face turned red as he realized that his plan was falling apart. This interloper was blocking his purchase of the golf course. And his chance to stick it to Vic Lewis. And embarrassing him in front of his daughter! He stood up and looked angrily at Don. "What do you care about these three and their lousy golf course?" he yelled.

Don remained seated and calmly pointed at Paul. "Thirty-eight years ago he carried me. Now I'm carrying him."

Dean desperately thought for a minute, then realized he had no more cards to play. "Screw all of you!" he screamed on his way out of the conference room. West got up to chase after his client, leaving all eyes on Rachel. She quietly gathered her things, gave Barry one last look, and left the room. He paused a beat, and then got up to follow her.

Rachel was standing in the hallway looking out the window. Barry walked over and leaned on the wall facing her. Neither spoke right away.

"So I guess you're keeping the golf course," Rachel said, still facing the window.

"Yeah, it looks that way."

"That's okay. I didn't really want to develop it into houses anyway."

"So that was the plan?" Barry asked.

"He thought we could make a lot of money together."

"And stick it to me, and to Uncle Vic, as well. Revenge for Dean Conrad."

"He's just looking out for me."

"Oh come on, Rachel. It's not about you, it's about him. He wants to always be your daddy, make you depend on him. And you let him. It's time to grow up."

Rachel turned to him. "You're one to talk about growing up! You have the same friends you had when you were 5 years old. Don't tell me to grow up."

They looked at each other for a moment, and then started laughing.

Barry said, "You're right. I am still hanging out with the same guys as when I was five." He walked over and sat down on a bench.

"You know, the reason I'm still friends with them is because I can count on them. They're there for me when I need them. Like right now, when I'm losing you."

Rachel came over and sat down next him. She let out a deep breath.

"You're right, too. I never really left my father's house. It's like I'm still a teenager." They sat looking straight ahead, and then Rachel said, "Speaking of teenagers, I hear you're dating one.

"She's not a teenager. She's 34. Oh, and she doesn't drive a white Corvette."

Rachel smiled and shook her head. "Yeah. I don't know what to do about Larry. I mean he's been chasing me for years. But he's still Larry. Same as when we were in college."

"You can do better."

She smiled. "That's what my dad says about you." She took Barry's hand. "But I'm not so sure anymore."

Barry turned to her. "Rachel, I want you to be happy. You know that I'll always love you."

Rachel looked at Barry with moist eyes, pulled her still jet black hair behind her ear, and smiled at him, her lower lip pausing just a split second before falling below her teeth. "I'll always love you, too."

64

It was almost dark when Tommy G drove the maintenance cart in from the far end of the course. Ironically, he had been repairing the fence not far from the hole he had used during his nocturnal forays. Plenty of noise was coming from the Northcroft clubhouse, and he burst into the room to find a raucous party.

"Tommy!" they all yelled.

"What's going on here?" he demanded.

Paul said, "We're celebrating our victory over the forces of evil! Have a drink!"

Tommy looked around the room. He recognized Frank and Kate, Paul and Julie, Barry and Jessica, Arthur Brinkman and who he assumed was Arthur's wife, and a large black man he didn't know.

Seeing his confusion, Frank offered, "Tommy, we kept control of the course today." Saluting Arthur with his glass, he said, "Thanks to our great attorney. Here's to Arthur!"

"To Arthur!"

Arthur pointed at Don. "Here's the real hero. Without him you'd have been sunk.

Paul said, "To Don Edwards, if you hadn't got shot, we'd have lost our golf course!"

"To Don getting shot!"

"And since Tommy's here," said Paul. "Here's to Tommy G, the heart and soul of Northcroft!"

"To Tommy G!"

Jessica handed Tommy a beer. "To Northcroft!" he offered.

"To Northcroft!"

As the party continued, Frank wandered over to Jessica.

"I want you to know that I think what you're doing with Barry is fantastic."

"What does that mean?" she asked defensively.

"I mean he's hitting the ball great. He shot 81 with us yesterday," Frank said innocently.

"Oh. Yeah, he's a good student."

"He's a good man," Frank said.

"What does that mean?"

Frank was amused at her phony indignation but didn't let on. "I mean I've known him all his life and he's a good man."

"Oh. Yeah. I guess."

"Anyway, keep up the good work."

"What does that...."

But Frank was already walking away, smiling.

Don was especially enjoying himself as the hero of the day. The salesmanship that made his car dealerships a success was on full display as he put his arm around each man to make his points, lowered his head in a sincere pose when talking quietly with the women. It was a good thing that none of them were in the market for a car or truck;

they wouldn't have stood a chance. Don had originally intended on driving back to Detroit that night, but Kate made him promise to spend the night at their house and leave in the morning.

The party ran out of steam about 12:30am, and Frank reminded everyone to respect the neighbors as they departed. He hoped to avoid another encounter with Mrs. McCauley.

65

Kate was in the kitchen the next morning when Don came down the stairs.

"Good morning," she said. "Coffee?"

"Please."

"How do you take it?"

"Just a little cream and sweet n low, if you have it. My wife is very strict with me these days."

"Well, we want you around a long time, Don. Frank went to get some donuts."

"No! Not donuts!" He held up his hands. "That's my weakness."

"We'll keep it a secret. Plus donuts are good for soaking up the alcohol from last night."

Don smiled. "Yeah. That was a great party."

Kate sat down at the table facing Don. "I just want you to know how much it meant to Frank that you were willing to invest like that. It's been a tough time for us and this really helped."

"It's a tough time for everyone, with this recession. Sales have been really slow at the car dealerships," Don said. "But you know, when things look bad I just look back on my life, and what might have been," he shook his head, "and I just feel blessed to be alive every day."

Frank came in through the garage door, carrying the box of donuts.

"Well look who's finally up," Frank said.

"Don says he doesn't want any donuts," Kate kidded.

"No donuts, Don?" Frank opened the box and walked over to tempt Don.

"I didn't say that. I said my wife doesn't want me to have any donuts."

"I've got a nice vanilla sprinkled with your name on it."

"Nah, if I'm going down, it will be with the chocolate long john."

Frank grabbed a blueberry cake donut and sat across the kitchen table from Don. "What's your plan today?"

"After breakfast I was going to hop in the shower and then hit the road."

"How would you like to be the hero again?" Frank asked.

Don sat back in his chair, smiling like a salesman who knows when he's being sold to. "Paul's the hero. All I did was invest in a golf course with a dynamic new management team."

Frank smiled. "Fair enough. But if you're willing to make a detour up to Milwaukee, I have a job you might be interested in."

There's an old joke about there being two seasons in Chicago – winter season and construction season – and Don saw plenty of orange road signs on his way up I-94 and into Milwaukee. Of course, his Chevy Tahoe sported all available upgrades, including the navigation system, and he was able to find street parking in downtown just a block from Styskal Jewelers. He made sure his pistol was stowed under his seat and out of eyesight before he climbed out of the SUV.

The bell sounded on the door, and the three people working the counter – two women and a man – plus an older woman customer turned to see who had entered. Probably don't get a lot of brothers in this store, Don thought. The man, Brad Taylor, approached him without a smile.

"Can I help you?"

"Actually, I was referred to Kristen. Is she available?" Don said.

Brad turned around and a younger woman walked down behind the counter. "I'm Kristen."

Don smiled and offered his hand, which Kristen shook without a smile. "My name is Don Edwards. Would it be possible to speak to you over by the watches?"

"Sure," she said, and they moved over to the left display cases under the watchful eye of Brad, the other worker.

"Are you interested in a watch, Mr. Edwards?" she said.

"You certainly have some nice ones here. But first I'd like to talk to you about Paul Smith."

Kristen took a step back and crossed her arms. "Really."

"I'm not asking you for anything other than to listen to my story. You're a grown woman and can make your own decisions."

"Decisions about what?" she looked around the store. Brad was in the back right corner of the store and not even pretending that he wasn't watching them.

"Your dad is getting married next month."

"No kidding."

"No kidding."

"What does that have to do with you?" she asked.

"Well, I have a little story to tell you," Don said, and he told Paul's daughter about her father carrying a wounded soldier through that field back in 1970. "Of course, I was much thinner then," he laughed.

Don was an expert at reading people. He saw that Kristen had never heard that story before, and that it resonated, but he also saw that there was plenty of what he assumed was resentment that had accumulated over the years. This would not be an easy sell.

"So he sent you up here to invite me to his wedding, is that it?"

Don shook his head. "No, not at all. He doesn't even know I'm here."

"So how'd you find me then?"

"Frank Jordan suggested I talk to you."

"I see," she said. "So Mr. Jordan sent you up here."

"Look, I'm sure that your dad wasn't..."

"You're right. He wasn't." Kristen interrupted. "He wasn't there for me, he wasn't a good husband to my mom, he wasn't a lot of things."

Don held up his hands in surrender. "You're right, he probably was a bad father. I'm not here to tell you different."

"Good."

"Look, all I came here to do is tell you that I owe my life to your dad. When you get to be my age you look at things differently. My dad wasn't around much when I was growing up, and when he was, I was terrified of him. He was plenty tough on me and my brothers and sisters. He had no education. He didn't know any other way. I didn't even cry when he died.

"But if I had the opportunity to talk to him today, I'd tell him that I understand. I'd tell him that I know he did the best he could. I'd just like to have that opportunity. That's all."

Kristen wiped her eyes. "You don't understand."

"No, I don't understand. Your life is your life. All I'm here to do is give you the opportunity to see and talk to your dad again. It's an opportunity I wish I had. And someday, you may wish you had it, too."

Kristen looked out the front window. "I appreciate you coming. I'm not sure I can do what you're asking."

"That's up to you." Don extended his hand. When Kristen offered hers he took it in both of his hands. "It was a special treat to meet you. Thanks for listening to my story."

He exited the store, climbed back into the Chevy, and headed home to Detroit, Michigan.

66

After sending the 6:45 am group off the first tee Frank
had a gap until 7:05. He sat down on the bench and looked
out over Northcroft Golf Course. It was a perfect late
summer day with just enough breeze to keep things cool.
Was this the life he wanted? If he turned down Walter's
hedge fund job he was out – there would be no return to
Wall Street.

The money he could make at Northcroft in the near
term was uncertain, although when – and if – the economy
recovered they could probably make a big payday by selling
the course down the road. Of course there were no
guarantees in the hedge fund business either, although he
knew plenty of guys that had made a fortune in a very short
period of time. Kate would support him whatever he did –
she was like that – so this was his decision, and it was a big
one.

It would be tough to bail on Paul and Barry, but was
that enough to pass up what could be a hedge fund pot of
gold at the end of the rainbow? Besides, they're both
capable, they could handle it. Of course, Paul had quit
being an electrician, a job he was very good at and liked, to
take a flyer on running the golf course with him. Barry's life
was topsy-turvy, with a marriage ending, a new romance

with a younger woman starting, and he had made a big career gamble, as well. Certainly there was value in working with his lifelong friends, and being an owner... But that hedge fund money, that could truly be life-changing.

Frank called Jimmy Boyle on the walkie-talkie. "Hey, Jimmy?"

"Yes, Frank?"

"Take over as the starter for a few minutes. I have to go inside to make a phone call."

He closed his office door, took a deep breath, and dialed Walter Reilly.

Jessica walked out to the driving range with her new client, Tammy.

"Have you played before?"

"No, this is my first lesson. My husband loves the game, so I thought I'd give it a try. Although we're separated now," Tammy said.

Jessica thought that was an odd thing to share right off the bat, but people say all kinds of things at a golf lesson, although typically it's more like, "I usually hit the ball better," or, "I don't know why I'm so bad today." Jessica never understood that, since getting better was the whole point of the lesson and she couldn't fix a swing unless she knew what was broken. Why did the student think they had to play well at the beginning of the lesson? The golf pro wasn't there to judge them; they were there to help them play better.

"Let's start at the basics," Jessica said, and helped Tammy with her grip and stance. Then she showed her how to take the club back, shifting the weight to the right leg, and start the downswing.

"You really have a nice manner about you," Tammy said. "What's your background?"

"You mean where did I play in college?"

"Sure, that. But how did you get interested in golf in the first place?"

"Mostly from my dad, he used to take me to the range when I was little. Here, let's hit a few and see what we have."

Tammy addressed the ball. "Yes, daughters like to please their fathers. That I can relate to." She topped the first ball she hit, then hit too far behind the second one.

"That's okay, you'll get the hang of it. Let's remember to shift our weight back, then forward."

"Did you grow up around here?" Tammy asked.

"Actually in a suburb of Indianapolis. I played at IU."

"Oh, some of my son's friends went to Indiana. Did you become a golf pro right after?"

"No it takes a bit to get certified. Let's hit a few right at that yellow flag out there. That's about 75 yards."

Tammy topped a couple more, then hit a decent shot just to the left of the flag.
"Hey!" she shouted.

"That was great, Tammy. Let's do that again."

"You're a great teacher. Very patient. You must have children?"

"No, no children. This job makes you patient."

"I couldn't do it. You must have to deal with all sorts of rude people," Tammy said. "Plus you probably get hit on all the time."

Jessica suddenly wondered if that was what was happening now. Tammy – what did she say her last name was, Wynette? – was very pretty and fit, about 55, Jessica estimated, with long dark hair and an unusual smile. Jessica didn't want to jump to conclusions – some students were just naturally chatty – but few were quite so interested in her personal life.

"Let's try to hit that yellow flag again. Remember about the weight shift," she said.

Paul pulled up in his golf cart to the first tee, where Frank was talking to the next foursome to tee off. When he finished, Frank walked over to Paul's cart. "How's the 14th fairway looking?"

"Still needs a little work but that Tommy's a genius. Without him we'd be calling this Northcroft Parking Lot by now," Paul said.

"Yeah, he's the real deal," Frank said. His gaze drifted over to the driving range and he spotted Jessica with her new student. "Now there's something you don't see every day," he said.

"What's that, Frank?"

"Jessica Weaver giving a lesson to Rachel Stone."

"What?!" Paul jumped out of the cart to see. Frank was already jogging to the clubhouse.

Jessica and "Tammy Wynette" were walking back from the range and were 20 yards from the clubhouse when Barry got to the door. The women saw him and kept on walking, while he stopped and looked at them with a "What's wrong with this picture?" expression.

Rachel smiled at him and turned to Jessica. "Thanks for the lesson. It was a pleasure to meet you." As she walked past Barry on the way to the parking lot she said, "She's very nice. Good luck."

Barry was speechless as he turned and watched her walk to her car. Jessica came up beside him. "What was that all about? Barry?"

He continued to watch Rachel walk to her car.

"Barry? Hello?"

"That was Rachel," he said without averting his gaze.

"That was Rachel?! She said her name was Tammy something. Tammy Wynette."

"Tammy Wynette was an old time country and western singer. Her big hit song was called "*Stand By Your Man.*"

Barry and Jessica walked up to the big tent where the Deer Lake Library used book sale was going on. An older gentleman blocked their entrance.

"I'm sorry, sir. Today is the presale for Supporters of the Deer Lake Library Association. The regular sale begins tomorrow and goes through Sunday."

"I see," Barry said. "Well, I love libraries and live in the district. Can I join today?"

Sure, there's a table right over there."

"How much does it cost?"

"It's 15 dollars for an individual membership and 25 dollars for a family membership."

"Great. That's a worthy cause," Barry said. "I'll be right back."

"I still can't let you in today," the man said. "You have to have already been a member."

"I don't understand. You want to add members, right?"

"Of course."

"Well I'm willing to join right now if I can go in buy some books."

"No, you have to have been a member before today."

"Well, let's think this through," Barry said. "If I become a member today, I'll buy lots of books today. I'm already here today. But if I have to come back tomorrow then I won't join, and I won't buy lots of books. Doesn't it make more sense to let me join and go in today?"

"This is the presale day for current members only," the man said.

Jessica nudged Barry, and he looked at her and smiled.

"I understand," he said. "Thank you for your time." And he and Jessica walked away.

68

Paul was filling in at the pro shop desk taking payment for greens fees when he happened to notice the name on the Black American Express card.

"Walter Reilly. You're a friend of Frank's, right?"

"I am. Frank and I worked together years ago. Is he around?" Walter asked.

"He's running an errand. He'll be back in about an hour. I'm Paul Smith, one of Frank's partners."

"Oh, congratulations. You guys must be doing really well," Walter said.

"We're doing all right."

"You must be doing way better than that. Frank turned down a chance for big money at a hedge fund." Walter slipped his credit card back into his wallet. "I'm going to go warm up. Tell Frank I'll try to catch him at the turn."

Paul watched him exit the pro shop. Well, I'll be damned, he thought.

69

October, 2008

Any cars pulling into the Northcroft parking lot on Saturday night after 6pm were greeted with a sign:

COURSE CLOSED FOR WEDDING. PLEASE COME BACK TOMORROW

A white trellis adorned with Julie's favorite flowers was set up on the tenth fairway, with rows of white folding chairs on either side of the aisle. A deal had been made with Reverend Dean, an avid golfer, to perform the ceremony in exchange for 8 free rounds. Music was provided by Jason The Keyboardist, an avid tennis player, who had to be paid in cash.

The wedding was to take place at 7:15pm, Julie's favorite time of day, when the shadows from the big oak trees to the west would frame the setting like a picture.

Barry was making sure everything was ready – that the power to the keyboard and speakers were hooked up, that the caterer had the food in the clubhouse, that the drinks were on ice, and that the automatic sprinklers were manually shut off. Standing over the sprinkler knob he thought just for a moment about playing the ultimate prank on Paul, but he couldn't do that to Julie. Paul, you're lucky

I'm a good friend, he thought, as he twisted the knob to the off position.

Inside the clubhouse, the groom was concerned about one of the guests.   "Frank, where's Don?" Paul asked. "It's seven twenty."

"I don't know. Maybe I-94 was bad. He said he had to pick something up. "

"I told him to drive here yesterday."

"Yes, that would've been the way to go. He'll be here, don't worry," Frank said.

"It's your big day, he won't miss it."

"All right." Paul took a deep breath. "Let's do this."

Jason The Keyboardist started with the traditional *Pachelbel Canon in D,* and the three men assembled to the left of the preacher. Julie's friend Elaine and her daughter Sandra walked gracefully down the aisle to balance out the other side. Coming out of the clubhouse, Julie looked so happy she was almost crying as she walked down the aisle in a light blue dress. When she got to Paul they turned to face each other, and Reverend Dean began the service.

Prior to the vows and ring exchange he said, "Paul and Julie have asked Thomas G to share some thoughts today. Thomas?"

Tommy Gianelli walked up and took Reverend Dean's place. It was the first time anyone there had seen him in a suit, and an Armani suit at that, which naturally restarted the speculation of just how much money he had. He reached into his coat jacket and pulled out some note cards.

"When you spend all day at a golf course, you see a lot. At the beginning, it's just you and the ball. Nothing happens until you initiate the action, take your best swing, and then you must follow where the shot takes you. Sometimes, it leads you into the bright sunshine in the middle of the fairway. Sometimes it takes you into the woods, or the tall grass, and then you have to find your way out before you can resume your journey. If your shot takes you too far off your path, or into deep water, you may lose your ball, and have to start over with another. Sometimes even a well-struck shot ends up in the sand - so close to your destination - but you must again find your way out. Once on the green, the focus of your effort becomes more refined – a cup of 6 inch diameter – and the method of getting there requires finesse and accuracy, rather than power. The game requires that delicate balance of strength and precision, confidence tempered with respect. It is played in the elements the Earth provides – heat, rain, cold, wind. Other players compete with you, but each shot is yours to make. There are rules, and it is up to the individual's honor to abide by them. Each hole is a journey, and journeys are best taken together with those you love."

Tommy folded up his notes, smiled at the bride and groom, and took his seat.

No one objected to their marriage, and Reverend Dean pronounced them man and wife. "You may kiss the bride."

Just as Paul and Julie turned to walk back down the aisle, a sparkling green Chevy truck drove out of the parking lot and onto the fairway, honking its horn. It was covered in flowers and "just married" was written across the back window. The truck swerved to a stop just 15 yards from the newlyweds, and out stepped Don, who went around the other side to help his wife Ruthie out of the passenger side.

Surprise turned to laughter as the guests realized what was happening.

"What did you do?" Paul said.

"It's a wedding present. You can't drive that ratty old van, now that you're married to Julie."

Ruthie walked over and gave Julie a big hug. "Congratulations. We're so happy for you."

Julie managed a disoriented, "Thank you."

"My husband likes to make a big entrance," Ruthie said as she rolled her eyes at Don.

"Mission accomplished," said Paul.

Jason The Keyboardist hit the opening notes to the Rolling Stones' *Start Me Up*, and the party was on.

Chris Keller ended up giving one guest after another a quick swing evaluation, done in his suit and without the benefit of a golf club, but after all the lean years at Northcroft, he didn't seem to mind. Jessica avoided a similar fate by wisely clinging to Barry as he ran around making sure everything ran smoothly. When it looked like no major catastrophes were imminent, he sat down at a table, exhaled, and clasped her hand.

"Looks like you pulled off the social event of the season," she said.

"Yes, what formal affair is complete without a big green truck plowing up next to the alter?"

"I think that's a fabulous gesture. I just hope they decorated it here and didn't drive all the way from Detroit with those flowers. That would generate some unwanted attention."

"Don't worry. I think Don is always packing heat."

Jessica put her arms around Barry. "So, Mr. Stone, what do you think of your new life?"

"Well, let's see. My money is stuck in this stupid golf course, I'm living in my friend's spare bedroom, and I'm pushing all my iron shots to the right."

"Because you're too stubborn to change your grip," she said.

"No, that's not it."

"Really? Okay, what is then?"

Barry kissed her. "I do it on purpose. It gives me a reason to keep taking lessons from you."

Paul and Julie made their way through the party and found Uncle Vic. "Uncle Vic, thank you so much for coming. I wanted to introduce you to my bride."

"Congratulations," Vic said. "You know, I've known this character and his friends almost their whole lives. Feel free to call me if you need some advice on dealing with him. Or them. I think they come as a package deal."

"Believe me, I've seen how the three of them stick together," Julie said.

"I don't even like those guys," Paul said. "They just keep following me around."

Julie turned to Uncle Vic. "I'm so glad you came. Paul thinks so highly of you. It's really special to have you here."

"I wouldn't miss it. You look so beautiful." He turned to Paul. "And you're not half bad either in that outfit."

Julie gave Vic a big hug and kiss and they continued greeting the guests.

Paul's childhood friend Rick walked up to Uncle Vic.

"Richard. It's good to see you," Vic said.

"So Paul is finally tying the knot again," Rick said. "I never thought I'd see the day."

"I guess he found the right woman."

"Tough times to be getting married in, though. I mean, I think this recession is going to last a long time. A long time. I don't think the stock market will recover for years," Rick said.

Vic smiled. "I wouldn't be so sure, Richard. The stock market in 2009 might surprise you."

Kate Jordan was talking with Ruth Edwards about school systems, as Don sidled up to Frank and whispered, "Looks like my trip to Milwaukee was in vain."

Frank said, "Yeah, Kristen didn't show. There's a lot of baggage there, Don. It has nothing to do with you."

"Well, maybe I planted a seed," Don said. "You never know. Sometimes kids take a while to come around."

"I hope so."

"Me, too. I'd hate to think I've lost my touch as a salesman."

Jason was unplugging wires and loading his keyboard into its large vinyl case, the caterers were wrapping the leftovers, and the crew was folding up the white chairs to put on the carts. In a circle stood the bride and groom, Frank and Kate Jordan, Barry Stone and Jessica Weaver, Don and Ruth Edwards, and Tommy G.

Frank looked at Don and said, "I hope you guys will come over here often. It's an easy drive and I know a great assistant pro to fix your game." Jessica smiled.

Don laughed. "Oh, I'll be here plenty to check on my investment. Don't think that because I'm in Detroit that you can violate that debt ratio covenant. No sir."

Paul said, "Debt ratio? Without me your big ass would be lying in a rice paddy ten thousand miles from here. Don't give me any 'debt ratio!'"

"Fair enough," Don said. He embraced Paul. "I'm glad I found you, man."

"I'm glad you found me, too, man."

Tommy G said, "Can I say something?"

Everyone looked at him.

"Get that damn truck off my fairway!"

Epilogue

September, 2015

As another long, straight drive shot down the fairway, Jessica Weaver smiled at her student.

"You're hitting the ball great today," she said. "Your swing looks really good."

"I have been playing better recently. I think setting my wrists a little earlier is making a difference."

"You want to hit a few more, Tammy?" Jessica asked.

"No, that's enough," Rachel said. "I'm tired."

She slid the driver back in the bag and they started walking back to the clubhouse.

"Are you really going to keep calling me 'Tammy'?" Rachel asked.

"Yep," Jessica replied.

Rachel set her bag down outside the clubhouse and they walked into Barry's office.

"How'd it go?" he asked.

"She'd be ready for the LPGA tour," Jessica said. "If we could only improve her short game."

"I believe it," he said.

Rachel sat down at Barry's desk. "Oh, sure," she scoffed.

"I have to go. Mr. Campbell wants a lesson on getting out of the bunker," Jessica said. "When I come back in I'll be covered in sand." She looked at Rachel. "We on next Thursday?"

"We're on."

Jessica left, and Barry turned to Rachel. "She still calling you Tammy?"

"Still calling me Tammy."

"Yeah, she tends to hold on to things like that. It can be kind of annoying sometimes."

Rachel said, "Derek's coming home on Saturday. I thought we could all go out to Franco's that night."

"That sounds great. Is Dr. Jack coming?"

Three years ago Rachel had married Jack Feldman, a gastro-intestinal specialist.

"Jack's coming, so bring Jessica."

"I like Dr. Jack. He's good to have around when you go out to eat in case you have some bad shellfish, or something."

"Funny," Rachel said, standing up to leave. "Just be there at 7:30."

Barry walked around the desk and gave Rachel a hug. "See you Saturday."

Frank sat on the bench at the 1st tee talking on his iPhone as the late afternoon shadows lengthened.

"I understand that, but we're already running three courses," he said.

Paul came and sat down on the bench next to him, hearing only half the conversation.

"The car business is different. Yes, I'd like to make more money. Fine, I'll talk to Paul and Barry. No, I will. I said I will. Okay. All right. Best to Ruth." He pushed the button to end the call.

"Don't tell me, Don wants to buy another golf course," Paul said.

"He's called and texted four times today. He's relentless."

"I should've left him in that field."

Tommy G drove by in a maintenance cart filled with sand. He stopped in front of the two men relaxing on the bench, and said, "Must be nice to be the owners," before driving off.

Frank said, "He says that, but I still think he has more money than either of us."

"Maybe not," Paul said. "If we could actually sell Northcroft for what Arthur told us it was worth."

"You want to sell Northcroft?"

"No, I'm just saying…"

"You want to talk about real money?" Frank said. "I talked to my friend Walter Reilly yesterday. Remember that hedge fund job he wanted me to take, the one I passed on? He said they now manage just over a billion dollars in assets."

"Seriously?"

"It doesn't get any more serious than that."

"So what would your share of that be worth?" Paul asked.

"I don't even want to think about it."

Barry walked out of the clubhouse, stooped to pick up a sandwich wrapper and put it in the trash, and joined the other two on the bench. "Cubs are in St. Louis tonight. I have to run over and catch the game with Uncle Vic. That reminds me, I've gotta stop at Sunset Foods on my way."

"How's he doing?"

"He never changes. Still goes to work every day. Still tries to help people. You know, when Dean Conrad died he funded a caddy scholarship at Bellwood in Dean's name. Believe me, no one else was going to step up and do that."

"Uncle Vic, he's one of a kind," Paul said. "Okay if I head out? Julie and I are going to pick out some new bedroom furniture."

"Your first bed is in the divorcee hall of fame, isn't it?" Frank said.

"Come on, I've been with Julie for seven years," Paul said. "Enough is enough."

"All right, all right. And I'll close up here," Frank said.

Barry said, "I'll walk out with you," and he and Paul headed to the parking lot.

Frank sat on the bench watching his two friends walk away.

Acknowledgements

Special thanks to John Raffles, Andrea Raffles, Hannah Richards, Sean Millican, and Bob Macdonald, for suffering through the original drafts of this book. Thanks to my friend Ridley Pearson, the greatest mystery writer today, for his encouragement and example. Thanks to my brother Scott for hours of joy on the golf course. And most of all, thanks to my wife, Cathy, for her constant support and love.

Cover design by Andrew Seay

ABOUT THE AUTHOR

Mark Raffles worked for 30 years in the investment business and is a lifelong fan of the Chicago Cubs. He resides in Lake Forest, Illinois.

57010232R00145